W9-BOB-824

The Fling

JULIAN F. THOMPSON

The Fling

HENRY HOLT AND COMPANY • *New York*

Henry Holt and Company, Inc.
Publishers since 1866
115 West 18th Street
New York, New York 10011

Henry Holt is a registered
trademark of Henry Holt and Company, Inc.

Published in Canada by Fitzhenry & Whiteside Ltd.,
195 Allstate Parkway, Markham, Ontario L3R 4T8.

Library of Congress Cataloging-in-Publication Data
Thompson, Julian F.
The fling / by Julian F. Thompson.
p. cm.
Summary: When three high-school friends are invited to live
briefly with a wealthy neighbor, their lives are changed by their
relationships with a mysterious "gardener."
[1. Friendship—Fiction. 2. Mentally ill—Fiction. 3. Suicide—Fiction.]
I. Title. PZ7.T371596Fi 1994 [Fic]—dc20 93-33812

ISBN 0-8050-2881-1
First Edition—1994
Printed in the United States of America on acid-free paper. ∞

10 9 8 7 6 5 4 3 2 1

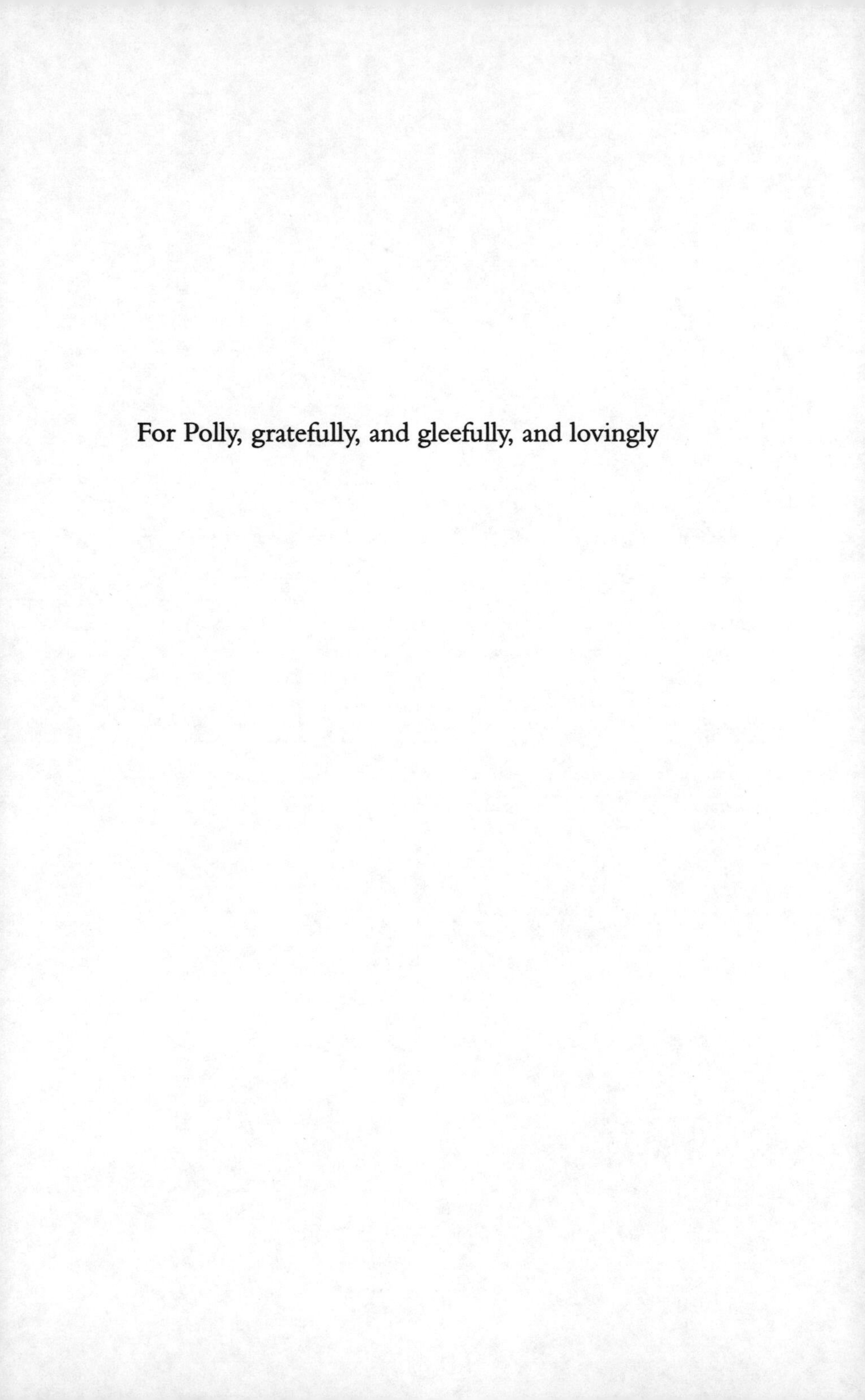

For Polly, gratefully, and gleefully, and lovingly

The Fling

My parents are extremely middle class and so, through no fault of their own, a handicap to me. Growing up, I always had enough to eat, a ruffled cliché of a room, and more clothes than I needed; I never suffered *want,* at all. Thus, my artistic growth was surely stunted.

The one, quite undeniably terrific, gift they gave to me (by accident? who knows?) was, yes, my name, *Felicia Gordon.* "A novel by Felicia Gordon"—wouldn't that look perfect on a cover? Yes; oh, *yes!* I plan to be a writer.

To compensate for my environment, I've worked . . . *assiduously*—right? On my vocab and other things. I think I generally look quite writerly. I'm tall and skinny, and I wear long skirts a lot. My hair is also long, and straight, and parted in the middle, and my eyebrows are unplucked and far apart. The color of my hair? Imagine me a horse: I'd be a bay. My face, however, is more oval, and my nose is small, my skin light-colored, smooth, and (as a rule) unblemished.

I have a slight astigmatism, which allows me to wear glasses, unaffectedly; when I do, they're round and small and wire-rimmed, and barely tinted, blue. When I don't, I have a wide-eyed, helpless, and unfocused look that may or may not be appealing.

I buy most of what I wear at Cleo's Closet; that's a thrift shop right in Northfield, my hometown. I buy enormous tops and sweaters. Clothes hang on me; I swim in them. My brother, Michael Gordon, was the captain of the swimming team in school. I learned self-discipline from watching him, the way he organized his life. My outerwear belies the true Felicia. But *under*wear—I buy it new, the sexier the better; I choose to keep the real me covered up. Many of my classmates call me Fleesh.

A lot of what I'm asked to do, as a junior at Northfield High, is an insulting waste of time. That isn't too original a comment. My brother used to make remarks like that out loud, so people said he was "intense," "undiplomatic," "pushy." He pushed off to college with another Northfield person, Riley Roux. They, and someone by the name of Jordan Paradise, are very actively opposed to nuclear weapons, and to war as a means of settling disputes. They network with a *myriad* (all right?) of other college students on these subjects; they have a new world order of their own in mind. I, by way of contrast, am completely apolitical. Michael was in love with Riley Roux, I'm pretty sure, but she picked Jordan Paradise to be her boyfriend. I wasn't in the least surprised. I was only twelve or so the first time I saw Jordan, but I swear to you: I *wanted* him. Not for anything *specific,* if you follow me, but overall, in general.

In any case, I do the work I'm asked to do in school, and though I sometimes sneer inside, I seldom make remarks about it. I love my brother, but I've no desire to be known as "Michael Gordon's sister."

He never would have taken Writing Workshop as a junior-year elective. But it's much my favorite class. What I hope to do in it is find my "voice," my *writer's* voice, that is. By that, I mean the way of writing that's uniquely me, the voice that best expresses me—my style, my personality, my way of looking at the world. Our teacher, Ms. Kevorkian, keeps saying we should never "compromise our own perceptions." *I* think what she means by that is "tell it like it is," and I try to follow all of her suggestions. A story that *she* wrote won first place in a college writing contest sponsored by some magazine. *Rolling Stone,* I think it was, but maybe it was *Seventeen.*

So, by way of introduction (me, to you) I thought I'd copy out the first couple of pages of a story I wrote recently, for Writing Workshop. Ready? Here we go:

Isn't She a Little Beauty?

by Felicia Gordon

Once you got adjusted to the whole *idea* of wearing one, the sign was not that big a deal, Amanda

Highstreet thought. It wasn't as if you were the only kid in town that had one on. And lots of kids who did were really *cool*. Comparatively few of them had been in, like, an accident.

Hers didn't go into a lot of detail. It simply said "For Sale," and then her parents' number. She usually pinned it on her shoulder bag, where it was obvious, but not *too* obvious. There was this one girl that she knew who'd walked around with not-too-big a sign she'd painted on a piece of white material and then sewn onto the seat of probably her tightest pair of jeans. But she'd been hassled by the cops for doing that. They made her parents take it off and put it somewhere else. Apparently, some idiot drove right up on the sidewalk, trying to read it, and he hurt his '92 Camaro pretty bad.

Of course, her folks had also advertised her in the paper. She thought she'd always remember the morning she came down to breakfast and found her parents composing the ad for the "Used Kids" section of the classifieds.

"Okay," her father was saying, "so far I got '1978 brunette, female, middle sized, decent shape, nice tan . . .' "

"I don't know if you want to say 'middle sized,' " her mother answered back. "That's kind of vague, it seems to me. But if you really think you ought to use it, write it all one word, like 'midsized.' That'll save you fifty cents. Isn't that right, Snookums, dear?"

This last was spoken to Amanda's mother's cat, a silky, sulky, long-haired Persian, whose special little chair, a Lay-Z-Kat, was drawn up to the table, right beside her mommy's.

"Is that about *me*?" Amanda said, pointing to the pad her dad was writing on. "You've decided to sell me, after all?"

"Possibly," her father said, "or maybe not. We'll have to see. Ed Fawbus, down at work, he told me that the market was real strong right now. Prices going through the roof. You know that Gloria of his? You won't believe it when I tell you what they got for her."

Amanda shook her head in disbelief. "Gloria *Fawbus*?" she said. "Someone paid good money for that clunker? Wait'll they try to get her to run down to the store, or something. . . ."

"Okay," her mother interrupted. "Suppose we keep on going here. It's nothing against you, Amanda, so just don't take it personal. You've been an okay kid for us. But Daddy needs new tires for the Jimmy, and he's got his heart set on them Goodyear Wranglers this time."

Amanda wasn't listening, however.

"Hey! What's that part meant to mean?" she asked, looking over her father's shoulder, and pointing. " 'Decent *shape*'? You mean my physical condition? Or you braggin' on my bod?"

"Either and/or both," her father said, unruffled by her attitude. He looked across the table at his wife. "No cavities?" he said. "You think I ought to put 'no cavities' in there? Or 'fully dentally inspected,' maybe?"

"No, 'decent shape' should cover medical and

dental both," Amanda's mother said. "It'll end up costing you a fortune, you try to put in everything. But I *would* add 'regular promotions, laundry, yard work.' And possibly . . ."

"Hold on a minute," said her dad. "I wanta check the Saab a sec. . . ." He got up from his chair and disappeared into the passageway that led into the attached three-car garage.

"Who's Mama's precious sweetheart?" said Amanda's mom to Snookums. "Would her like some fresh bay scallops for her breakfast, now?"

Amanda poured some cornflakes for herself, the supermarket's own generic brand. At least her folks had noticed her 'nice tan,' she thought.

"Boy, I can't get over that great wax job," said her father as he came back in the kitchen. "It really makes a difference when you have it done professionally, you know? And by a *Swedish* guy. But anyway—where were we?"

Please don't misunderstand. I'm not trying to tell you that's great writing, or anything like that. It's pretty rough—still needs a lot of work. Ms. Kevorkian was not too wild about that story.

But still. It's me, in certain ways, you know? The irony, for instance. And I actually do believe that some parents are a lot more interested in their cars and pets than they are in their kids. Not mine, of course. Oh, they gave *Michael* all sorts of freedom to go here and there whenever he wanted to, but they treat me more as if I am an . . . *I* don't know, *endangered species* of some sort. I can't do anything. That really hurts me, as a writer. I have a great need to experience all sorts of different things, a lot more than I have. You know that put-down people use, "Get a life"? Well, that could reasonably be said to me. I *need* a life; I really do.

Ms. Kevorkian keeps telling me I ought to practice modeling my characters on real people that I know, but to keep on using my imagination, plotting-wise, as I did in "Isn't She a Little Beauty?" So, I guess I will. As I said, I always try to follow her advice.

Two

I'm not so totally committed to my writing that I don't have any friends. I see other people lots, and I enjoy them. Besides, if I *did* go in my room and shut the door and write every day after school and on weekends, and not come out except for meals (not even all of them), I'd have my parents on my case, *instanter.* They view my writing as another phase I'm going through, and one that I'll grow out of. Being who they are, it isn't something that they'd tell the relatives about.

The most comforting and reassuring things I do for them

are those that make me appear to be "a typical American teenager." If I were able to, I would do more. But, sad to say, I don't need Clearasil, and dieting would be absurd. I *can* make a point of tying up the telephone from time to time, and once in a blue moon I force them to demand that I "turn the music down," but neither of those things comes thoughtlessly and easily to me. I suppose my greatest gift to them, the proof they must be doing something right, is my *complaining*—usually about some new attempt of theirs to keep me wrapped in cotton wool, as if I was some precious virgin of a china doll. This complaining, they assure me, constantly, "will get you nowhere." When I'm old enough to be "in your own house," they say, I can do whatever it is "until you're blue in the face." Then they usually add, "Just don't tell *us* about it."

But, yes, I *do* have friends, as I was saying. One rather interesting one is Allison Roux, the younger sister of that Riley Roux I mentioned—the girl I think my brother was in love with?

Allison is lots of things that I am not. She's gorgeous, to begin with, and has honey-blonde hair that just last month she had cut off so that it's now the length of Peter Pan's, or Joan of Arc's—or Maria's in *For Whom the Bell Tolls,* if you've ever read it. She's also an athlete, an All-Everything swimmer who'd draw a crowd every time she slipped into a tank suit, even if all she did was jump into the shallow end and do the deadman's float. In addition, she has parents who are *upper* upper class (by Northfield standards, anyway), and who (therefore? I don't know) allow her to do anything she wants to, just about. Their permission (or indifference) often comes long distance—they are always "on a trip," or just about to go on one, it seems to me. They sent their younger daughter off to boarding school in Massachusetts for her ninth-grade year, and though she said it was "okay," she decided she'd prefer to live at home thereafter and be a little more . . . *autonomous;* her parents, typically, agreed with this decision.

Allison has "had a life" for years and years, needless to say.

Because I know her well and think she is so interesting, I decided Allison would be a main character in my next short story—or novella, possibly. Ms. Kevorkian had wanted me to use "real" characters, remember? Of course, the first thing that I did was change her name, from Allison Roux to Annabel D. Day.

Here is how I started that new story (or, possibly, novella):

Sanctuary

by Felicia Gordon

Annabel D. Day made a practice of reading all of the graffiti in the girls' room's stalls at Southport High. It always amazed her how complicated and difficult the world appeared to be to many women more or less her age. By and large, their messages, inscribed in lead and ink and watercolor paint and maybe even blood, were questions and complaints about themselves and life in general. Sex and sexuality, bodily concerns (including eating and elimination disorders), teachers, and fellow students were all favorite topics. One day, in her junior year, Annabel was pleased to read a single forty-two-word exclamation that included all of those and was, in fact, a *curse,* whose object was a fairly well-known entertainer, unbeloved by women everywhere.

From time to time, she'd find a limerick or joke she liked [Question: Why does it take three women with PMS to change a light bulb? Answer (fiercely): Because it *does*!], but, as a rule, her girls' room reading wasn't memorable.

All that changed, however, on the eighth of April, when she saw the following, neatly printed rather high up on a left-hand wall:

Abused? Bummed Out? Abandoned?
Need a place to get away to?
Call 249-3253, for SANCTUARY

Annabel had her bag right in there in the stall with her, and so she wrote down the number on the back of her video rental card. She wrote "Sanctuary: 249-3253" in nice big letters with her black LePen. She wasn't abused, or bummed out, and she'd never thought of herself as *abandoned* (for heaven's sake), but she knew she wouldn't mind finding a place to stay while her parents were in Estoril this time. Someplace different from her mansion of a house, which was a long way out of town, let's face it.

That night, she called the number.

"Hello?" It was a woman's voice, the voice of a woman younger than her mother, but one whose wallet might contain the same impressive group of charge cards, Annabel inferred.

"Hello," said Annabel. "Sanctuary?"

"Possibly," the woman said. "It all depends."

"On who or what?" said Annabel.

"On you and whether you are serious," the woman answered. "Some girls call the number just for kicks, because it's there. To see if it's a joke, or something. It's like when boys find 'For an easy lay, call such-and-such a number' on a *boys'* room wall. Some kids call who wouldn't think of doing anything. *You* know the kind I mean."

"I guess," said Annabel, although she wasn't sure. Most boys she'd known, or heard about, seemed eager to do *everything*. "But me, I'm serious."

"I'll tell you what," the woman said. "If you're so serious—and you may be, you *sound* all right—you'll go down to the Unitarian church on Prospect Street after school tomorrow, by yourself. You know which one it is?"

"Sure," said Annabel. "The brick one, right on the corner there, on Main and Prospect. But what for? Is this some kind of test?"

"Sort of," said the woman, "but hold on a minute, I'm not done. When you get inside, follow the center aisle to the fourth pew from the front, on the left-hand side. Sit down in it and open the fourth song-book in, to the place where the marker is."

"Okay," said Annabel. "Fourth row on the left, fourth book in. I got it so far. Then what?"

"Maybe nothing," said the woman. "Maybe you'll feel inner peace and just forget this deal. In the old days, that's where people went for sanctuary—inside a church. You'll have to go and see what happens. That's if you're really serious."

"Stop saying that," said Annabel. "But look—you said it first. *Is* this, actually, a joke?"

"Absolutely not," the woman said. "It's a service I provide to kids—like you, conceivably. I own a huge old house, and I certainly *can* offer you some space in it, and food, for whatever length of time the two of us agree on. If I did, I'd ask you *not* to do some things, of course, while you were there, but aside from those, you'd be completely free to make your own decisions, when it comes to your own daily life."

"Not do *what*?" asked Annabel, suspiciously.

"Commonsense things," said the woman. "Drugs'd be a good example. Stuff that might imperil all of us. We can talk about that, if and when you ever get here. First of all, we'll have to see what happens at the church."

"Well," said Annabel, "this all seems pretty weird. But *probably* I'll go down to the church tomorrow, and do that fourth-row, fourth book stuff. And then, as you just said, we'll see."

"Fair enough," the woman said, and they hung up.

The next afternoon, after school, Annabel walked over to the Unitarian church, by herself, and into it, and down to the fourth pew to the left of the center aisle.

She looked around. She was the only person in the church, which smelled quite comfortably familiar—like Pledge, or maybe Murphy's Oil Soap. The interior was plain and simple; all the wood was either natural or painted white. She certainly felt safe enough in there, and reasonably peaceful.

The songbooks were in a rack on the back of the pew

in front of her. She took out the fourth one in and opened it to where the ribbon bookmark was.

On the left-hand page, there was "Amazing Grace," the music and the lyrics, both. On the right-hand page, the song was "Turn, Turn, Turn."

She did, of course, but only saw the same long rows of empty pews she'd noticed coming in.

"Hmmph," said Annabel. She stood up, turned into the center aisle, and left the church by the same door she'd come in by. But as she turned left on the sidewalk, to head back to where her car was parked behind the high school, she saw a dog, lying on its side beside a bush.

Her heart gave one great leap of apprehension. She feared the dog had been run over by a car, and then had dragged itself up by that bush to die. Annabel loved dogs, and children, and this dog was easily as big as a five-year-old. It appeared to be at least half chocolate Lab, with maybe Weimaraner blood as well. And possibly a fraction of Rhodesian ridgeback, and Chesapeake Bay retriever.

Then she saw the dog was breathing, and its eyes were open. There wasn't any blood that she could see, or evidence of broken bones. Annabel crouched down and ran a gentle palm along its big, brown, silky head. She was going to do whatever she could do for this fine-looking dog. She was going to *succor* him (or her).

The moment she had finished patting her (as it turned out), the dog sat up and tried to lick her face. The dog seemed fine; in fact, the dog was *smil-*

ing. She had a nice red collar on, and had been lying on her nylon leash.

Annabel reached for the two tags hanging from her collar, hoping she would find the dog's name, *and* her owner's name and phone number. She got one out of three, which isn't bad; the name of this big dog was printed on a round red tag, and it was Grace.

"Amazing," muttered Annabel, and smiled as she stood up, the red leash in her hand. The dog began to wag her tail and pull. She couldn't wait to go somewhere, it seemed, and take somebody with her.

At the time I wrote those pages—on a Tuesday, I believe it was—I didn't have a special sense about what I had done, at all. There wasn't any feeling of *momentousness*. I thought I'd made a promising beginning, simply. I'd taken my friend Allison and, in my mind, I'd made her into Annabel, my character. And if my plotline wasn't altogether likely, it was *possible,* at least.

With this story, I was trying out a new technique I'd heard about, from Ms. Kevorkian, of course. She'd told us how Ann Beattie writes. You've heard of her, I guess? The well-known short-story writer and novelist? A book of hers called *Chilly Scenes of Winter* was made into a movie. I try not to be impressed by movie credits, but . . . wouldn't that be *fabulous*? To have a book you'd done be faithfully produced and get to watch it in your own hometown?

But, anyway. What Beattie does, when she sits down to write (according to Ms. Kevorkian), is . . . just begin to *write*. No conscious planning goes on first. She doesn't do a line of any *out*line. She just lets whatever comes into her mind flow out, onto the page. After she's typed a little while—about two pages, as a rule—she reads what she has written and decides if it seems promising. If it does, she goes ahead and types some more; if it doesn't, off it flies into the trash, and she finds something else to do.

Ms. Kevorkian did not enthuse about this method. I suppose few writing teachers would. If *that* became the way to go, they'd all be out of work, I guess, except for criticizing. But I enjoy Ann Beattie's stories very much. I think she's really clever and insightful and . . . *oblique*. So I thought I'd try her way of doing things. If the story worked out well, I'd tell Kevorkian I'd done a six-page outline first—stayed up all night just working on the thing.

Four days after I had written what you read—the start of *Sanctuary*—I got a call from Allison. At that point, I hadn't yet made up my mind if I would tell her I was *using* her, or not.

"Hey, Fleesh," she said, "guess what."

"I can't; I won't," I said. "You have to tell me." Allie sometimes *milks* a moment till I feel like screaming.

"We're going to be, like, neighbors, just about," she babbled happily. "Starting Monday. Isn't that fantastic? *I'll* be living in the city, too!"

This was a little joke we shared. She liked to call our three-to-four-horse town "the city," possibly because I often called her house a "country manor."

"Come again?" I said. "You all are *moving*?"

"Not everyone," she said. "Just me. Short term. Mom and Dad are going to Puerto Vallarta for a month to stay with friends—or, not *actually* Puerto Vallarta, but *near* there. And me, I'm going to stay five blocks away from you, I think, on Sycamore. For maybe the entire time they're gone."

"Wow," I said. "How serendipitous. But tell me more, more facts, more *details*. Where on Sycamore exactly, and with whom? The Arnolds?" I hadn't made the least connection with my story yet.

"No, no. Hell, no." Allie made rude sounds, rude *yorking* sounds. "I'd never willingly reside with Josie-Posie—give me credit for a little taste, all right? But—you know the Grunfeld place? The huge house, set way back? Well, *there*. A woman named Kate Mycroft bought it—filthy rich and thirtysomething, but also used to be a dance teacher and really likes kids. I only met her yesterday—Mom had her out for a drink after tennis—and she told me she would *love* to have me stay at her place any time my folks were gone. And she really *meant* it, you could tell. She told me I could use her house as if it was my college *dorm,* or something—not that she actually thought I was in college, or anything. Isn't that fantastic? That I could have friends over, even have friends *stay,* that there absolutely was a ton of room." She paused to get a breath. "Isn't that the biggest break you ever heard of? Having my own city hideaway?"

That was the moment that it dawned on me.

"It's a *sanctuary,* isn't it?" I said. "Sort of like a sanctuary."

"I guess," she said. "Sort of. Except nobody's after me. But whatever you want to call it, I can't wait. It'll be a neat-o change for me to be in town and closer to . . . well, *people*."

Of course I wondered just which people Allie had in mind, beside myself. You never knew with Allie.

"This woman, this Kate Mycroft," I began; I had to know. "She have a dog, by any chance?"

"A dog?" said Allison. "I wouldn't know. I guess she might; she's certainly the *type* to have a dog, I'd say. I haven't been there yet; I'm dropping by tomorrow." She paused. "You want to come along and help me check it out? I'll pick you up." She laughed. "Then you can find out for yourself about the dog."

"Gee," I said. "I'd like to do that, sure. And if the setup meets my standards, possibly I'll go and stay there, too. I'm sure Muh-*mah* would *love* my doing that. She's always after me to try new things, get out on my own, live dangerously and freely, like the California condor or the golden eagle, right?"

Allison cracked up, of course. She knows my mom: Ms. Cool when I have company, but Warden Gordon once the visitors go home.

After we hung up, I told myself that it was just a huge coincidence: that I'd write something in a story and later sort of have it happen in real life. It also went to show how well I knew my friend and understood her situation. What I'd written in my story had been proven to be true-to-life.

Face it, I intend to be a writer someday, but I'm not a mover and a shaker yet. Felicia Gordon is a lovely name, but (as Mom's my witness!) not to be confused with "God."

Three

Next morning—it was Sunday—I used my Princess phone (my thirteenth-birthday present from guess who?) to call up Allison. The one thing that she hadn't said was *when* we'd go check out the Grunfeld/Mycroft situation.

Instead of Allie, I got Thalia. My father would have called her "the Rouxs' cook." *I* think of her as a cross between Julia Child, the Pythia, Golda Meir, and Mother Teresa—and in looks, an island queen, perhaps. Allie says she is "our major-doma."

"Hi, Thalia," I said. "It's me—Felicia. Any Allie-sightings yet, this morning?"

"Not so much as any *sound,* Felicia," she replied. "Let's see, what time is it? You got a quarter after ten? I don't look for her before eleven—but you can *talk* to her right now. I'll buzz her, if you say the word; you *know* I will."

It's a measure of Thalia's importance in the Roux household that Mr. Roux installed an unusual intercom system in the manor, years ago. Instead of all the master bedrooms having bell-pushes that activate a buzzer in the kitchen, this one goes the other way. *Thalia,* from the downstairs pantry, pushes one of seven different buttons (five bedrooms, study, sewing room); then, whoever's buzzed upstairs jumps quickly to the intercom and asks her what she wants.

"No," I said, "don't bother. It's just that she's picking me up on her way to the old Grunfeld house today, and she didn't tell me when that's going to be."

"Oh, I believe that *I* can tell you that," said Thalia. "It'll be after regular people's lunchtime. She said she told Kate Mycroft two o'clock, so I suspect that you can look for her about five minutes to."

"Copacetic," I responded. "I can't wait to see the setup over there. It sounds a little like the answer to a maiden's prayer. What do *you* think, Thalia?"

To say I value her opinions is an understatement. My mother's always saying, "You believe everyone but me."

"It may be *excellent,*" she said. "I'm off, myself, the first two weeks the Rouxs are going to be away, and I been telling them they ought to get someone to come and stay with her out here. But now there's this; it *could* be even better. She'd be near her friends, like you, especially, and have a change her*self.* Of course I can't say that I *know* Ms.

Mycroft, but she *seemed* all right, a real nice person. Commonsensical, but also *elegant,* you know?"

"Uh-huh," I said. I sort of did. It sounded like a worthwhile combination, one that lots of people might aspire to. Writers, though, are different. We/they are more *impulsive,* oftentimes a little *wild,* creatures of *emotion,* unconcerned with . . . well, *appearances* (oh, don't I wish?).

"I really want to meet her," I went on. "So, would you tell Al I called? And that I'll be waiting out in front at ten till two?"

"You bet I will, Felicia," Thalia said. "And don't forget to tell me all about it, later on, sometime."

"Oh, absolutely," I replied. Telling, after all, was one of my main things in life.

"I think that Ernie's down from college for the weekend," said my mother. "I can't *wait* to see him; he is such a *mess.* I told Marie *exactly* what was going to happen, when she let him have his ear pierced, in tenth grade. That's when it all began. From that point on, he just went . . ." She turned on the disposal, and it did its thing, gulping down its serving of potato peels. "Like that," my mother finished, with a gesture at the ugly sounds now coming from the sink.

It was about ten minutes after I had gotten off the phone with Thalia. I'd gone downstairs, and I was sitting at the kitchen table, eating what I almost always have for breakfast: orange juice, a toasted cinnamon-raisin bagel with peanut butter on it, and coffee. My mother was beginning to make potato salad for the family get-together at Aunt Marie's. Ernie was my cousin; he had recently taken part in a demonstration against a proposed nuclear power plant.

And, before that, he'd signed up for a summer workshop called "Getting Reacquainted With the Child in You." Either one of those, according to my father, was a certain sign of "ding-dongism."

"So, you going to go to church today?" my mother asked me. She was taking off this cover which had been over the biggest of the stove's four burners. My mother keeps a spotless kitchen—a spotless, *modest* kitchen, even. There are covers on the stove's burners, and she has hoods that go over the blender and the toaster. So you'd never know they *did* it, I suppose—or even got turned on.

"I think," I said. "I think I'll go to Mass down at St. Leo's."

"Um," my mother said.

She didn't quite know how to handle this religious "phase" of mine. She and my father went to the Methodist church, the biggest one in town, about four times a year. His family was Jewish, and she was raised a Catholic, but that was then and now is now, and most of the major players in Northfield are Protestants. Neither of them was what I'd label "spiritual," but they always had a "God bless you" ready for a sneeze, and they certainly couldn't bring themselves to *disapprove* of church attendance. I'd decided to sample all of the various religions represented in our town and see what each one had to offer a person like myself. Besides, familiarity with the Bible seemed to be one thing an awful lot of writers had in common.

"And I'm afraid I can't make lunch today," I said. "I've got to be someplace at two."

"What?" my mother said. She put the big pot of potatoes on the stove, then checked her hair and took a sponge and started to rub down the spotless countertop—again. My mother has short, tinted hair that's never out of place. I have my father's lanky build, thank God; my mother is a chunk.

"*Everybody's* going to be there," she informed me. "Benny, Lou, and their three little ones are coming up from Stratford. Aunt Loretta and her boyfriend's coming. Even that peculiar Kevin, Cousin Winthrop's boy? I'll bet you anything he's"—she extended her right hand, palm down, and, having spread its fingers, rocked it back and forth—"*you* know what I mean." My mother's such a paragon of subtlety—and homophobia. "But, anyway, where d'you have to go that's so important?"

"I'm going with Allison to see this place she may be staying at, while her parents are in Mexico," I said. "She asked me specially to come with her, sort of as an extra pair of eyes. It's the old Grunfeld house, on Sycamore; a woman named Kate Mycroft owns it now."

I suppose I *could* have gone to Aunt Marie's for lunch and run back here in time, but I really do despise these potluck get-togethers that my family goes in for. The women always get you off to one side and ask you *questions,* mostly about your social life, and the guys all try to make you play "a little volleyball."

"The *Grunfeld* house?" my mother said. I'd known that that would *pique* her interest. My mother is extremely social-conscious, if you know what I mean, although she has no social *conscience* whatsoever. "I *thought* someone had bought it. I saw *two* Simonetti trucks turn in there—what?—last month, I think it was." Simonetti Bros. are the big contractors here in town. "I wonder if they're totally redoing it, or what. And Allison may stay there, huh?"

"Could be," I said. "I think Mrs. Mycroft is a friend of her mother's. I know they play tennis together."

My mother nodded sagely. She approved of Allison, her sister, Riley, their parents, and their friends. And, by making Kate a "Mrs.," I'd established her respectability.

"I suppose that I can tell them all you've got the flu," my mother grumped. "Mrs. Raymond, down the street, said there were lots of people out where *she* works, down at the phone company. But couldn't you get Allison to make it later on, or something? The relatives all understand with Michael—he's so far away, at college. But you, they know you're home, and so they want to *see* you—what a beautiful young lady you've turned out to be—and hear how good you're doing, out of your own mouth. That's part of being *family,* that kind of give-and-take."

"Well, I *can't* get Allison to change the time," I said. "This is when Mrs. *Mycroft* said. Any relative who wants to give-and-take with me that much can call me on the phone."

"You kids!" my mother said disgustedly, but proudly, too. "Everything is phone-phone-phone, I swear to God. It doesn't even matter who you're talking to. It could be anyone—a wrong number, someone trying to reach . . . oh, I don't know, the *Pope*—and you'd still talk to them. And it's the same with calling up, you don't even have to *like* the person, you'll stay on for hours. Just wait'll you start getting your own phone bill. Then we'll see how long you . . ."

Continuing to mutter about my (largely imaginary) adolescent habits, my mother cruised around the kitchen, dabbing at (wholly imaginary) fingerprints and spills with her sponge. I finished up my breakfast, washed and dried and put away my dishes, and got out of there.

The old Grunfeld house is hidden from the street by

trees, a good-sized wooded area that was behind a low brick wall surmounted by a metal picket fence. Driving off the road and into this green tunnel, one had a sense of entering a wholly new domain, a place that wasn't part of Northfield life at all. At least that's what I said to my friend Allie.

"Yeah," she said. Allie had a taste for fantasy. "It looks like an enchanted forest. The sort of place that *unicorns* might live in, don't you think?"

It did, it did. Paths, whose surface seemed to be some soft material, like ground-up bark, meandered through it. I spotted resting places—wooden swings and benches—and a narrow, slowly flowing stream. I surmised that, farther on, there'd be a lovely crystal pool, the kind a princess would be pleased to sit beside, and maybe weave a garland out of dogwood blossoms.

As we approached the house, the woods gave way to lawns and flower beds; there were some low stone walls, and a gazebo. A level patch had wickets and two stakes on it, for croquet. I saw somebody walk into the woods with what appeared to be a stack of boards, balanced on one shoulder. The gamekeeper, perhaps, I thought. Maybe on his way to build a *bower* he could meet his girlfriend in (if not the lady of the house).

I'd seen the big old home—the mansion—once before, so it wasn't a surprise. One day, about a year ago, I'd motored up its gravel drive with—yes!—my *father,* of all unlikely people. We'd been coming back from somewhere (probably his favorite restaurant, a Pizza Hut), and he'd turned off the road and up the private drive (in a cloud of pepperoni-scented affability), saying only that he'd always had a hankering to see the place and Jed, this friend of his, a realtor, had said that it was presently unoccupied. I'd been a lot less interested, back then.

But since the time I'd seen the house, some things had happened to it. It was still enormous, of course—long, three-storied, with a sloping roof and steeply overhanging eaves—but the weathered shingles it once had for siding had been replaced by clean, white clapboards, and many of the windows now had dark green shutters hung beside them. The overall effect was to make the place look much more cheerful and, if anything, even more enormous than it used to be.

Chances are, the crunchy driveway heralded our coming. In any event, just as we pulled up beside the house, the front door opened, and Kate Mycroft came to greet us. And with her, bounding out in front of her, and barking, was a dog!

It wasn't Grace, however, by a long shot. This one was black and tan and white, about a third the size of the amazing one, and male; he also had a very different personality: aggressive, vocally at least. He turned out to be a friendly (if spirited) little thing, a Jack Russell terrier (I'd never heard of one before), who answered to the name of Roger.

Kate Mycroft struck me as a perfect match for her surroundings. She looked at ease, and rich, and gracious, and (yes, exactly, Thalia) "elegant." That she managed that while wearing shorts (white linen ones) and a fitted, turquoise, sleeveless camp shirt is testimony to the length of her tan legs and the perfection of her blonde pageboy. And maybe the fact that she treated this gigantic mansion of a house as if it were the little Cape across the street from my place.

"Welcome to our brand-new paint job," she called out as we debarked from Allie's bright red 'stang convertible.

“Doesn’t it look spiffy? And, please, pay no attention to this *monster* of a dog. Hush, Roger, will you, dammit?” She shook hands with Allison, who turned toward me and said, “Felicia Gordon.”

“Hi, Felicia. Glad that you could come. Please call me Kate,” Kate said, and shook with me. She had a penetrating gaze, I learned, and hazel eyes, and one of those standard-featured, Waspy faces. But she wasn’t in the least bit *bland*. She looked at people with a great intensity, as if she thought they possibly might have something she wanted, like the secrets of the universe, perhaps. We went inside with her and Roger.

We never did sit down (except for Roger). Kate took us on a tour, beginning right away, though it was not a hurried one. Before it ended, we had looked in almost all the rooms; from time to time, we’d stop and chat while standing in one place, or leaning back against a wall.

Kate asked a lot of questions, but she also volunteered a lot about herself. Before we left, she learned that Allison and I loved animals of almost every sort, that both of us were apt to cry at movies, that we didn’t drink, adored the way her woods looked, driving in, and had raised almost two thousand dollars at school to help the needy Kurds and Bangladeshis. We, for our part, found out she’d always lived in the Midwest before, had worked as a copywriter in an ad agency as well as as a dance teacher, had vague thoughts about turning the house into a health spa or a convalescent center someday, had recently broken up with a longtime boyfriend, and loved the idea of having someone like Allison staying in the house.

“A big place like this needs noise and laughter in it, don’t you think?” she said.

The living arrangements that she had in mind seemed

nothing short of heavenly, to me. Allison would basically have her own part of the house, what formerly had been the servants' end of it (or "wing," as I preferred to say). Their bedrooms had been on the second and third floors of the left-hand side of the house, directly over the humongous kitchen, the pantry, the servants' dining room, and the servants' sitting room. And there were eight such rooms for Al to choose from! As Kate Mycroft told it, in the old days, when the house was built, the "staff" would probably have consisted of a butler, a chauffeur, a cook, a laundress, and at least four maids. The gardeners, she explained, would probably have been local men, who came in by the day. Now, however (she went on), the "staff" consisted of one cleaning lady, who was there two days a week.

"I thought that we could get our own breakfasts and lunches," Kate said to Allie, "and we could more or less join forces for dinner. Unless you're going out, or something. We could check each other out, each morning. I'll take care of the shopping. We can keep a list going in the pantry, and you can write down stuff you want or need."

Allison was wreathed in smiles throughout the tour; who wouldn't be? The former servants' rooms were smaller than the "master" bedrooms on Kate's side of the house, but they were far from crummy or . . . *demeaning*. And it was neat how she could have this sort of section of her own. The room that Allie chose as hers must have been set up for a married cook and butler, once upon a time, because it had a double bed (taking up a lot of the floor space) with a nice quilt on it, a hooked rug on the floor, and a perfectly respectable maple chest of drawers. There even was a painting on the wall, of two pears and some grapes, beside a burnished copper bowl.

As we were leaving, Allison suggested that she move in Thursday, if that'd be all right; clearly, she'd been so impressed she didn't feel the need to ask for my opinion of the setup.

Kate said that'd be just great. Possibly because they both had lots of money, they seemed totally relaxed with each other. Watching them, the way they smiled and even touched each other, I thought they looked like dear old friends, already.

Four

I don't know if I should call Allie's move into Kate Mycroft's house a minor pain in the ass or not. Maybe I should substitute "behind" or "butt" for "ass," and act as if I never use vulgarities, or even think them.

But wouldn't that be hypocritical of me? Yes, absolutely; yes. And would a *writer* do a thing like that? Never, if she hoped to have a shred of self-respect.

And so the phrase, and sentence, stands.

I should admit, however, that her doing what she did was

both a pleasure *and* a pain, to me. On the one hand, I was *very* pleased to have her be in town, in easy walking distance from my house. Not only that, but she was also in a situation where she could have visitors (such as myself and groups of others), without first going through familial red tape.

So, from the point of view of friendly "Fleesh," the fun- and life-starved girlfriend, it was great to have Al settled in the Mycroft residence.

But for Felicia Gordon, fiction writer, Allie's move was something of a complication—yes, even exactly what I said it was. F.G. was working on a piece about a high-school junior, Annabel D. Day, who planned to leave her home and live in someone else's house, a stranger's, and have some . . . *interesting* adventures there. But now the writer's friend, Allison Roux (who was admittedly the model for Annabel D. Day, which was another complication), had gone and done exactly what A.D. had done. And Allison, as Felicia Gordon well knew, was perfectly capable of having—yea, *creating*—an even more interesting set of adventures than those a not-especially-experienced writer could think up for *Annabel* to have.

Suppose that happened—then what? It was already tempting to use descriptions of Kate Mycroft and the Grunfeld house—true things I'd seen—just stick them in my story. And then, as various other things happened to Allison (and whoever else became involved in "life" at Mycroft House), I could put them in, too.

But Felicia Gordon wasn't a *biographer*. Nor did she do—what is that loathsome word? *novelizations?*—where the writer sort of fills in the blanks, turning big events in other people's lives (or someone else's screenplay, even) into a "story."

I had to take a stand, protect my literary integrity.

So, in the second section of my novella, *Sanctuary,* written Sunday night, I made sure that characters and settings were quite different from anything I'd seen earlier that day.

I had Grace, the big brown dog, lead Annabel up the steep hillside that my fictional town of Southport was built on (Northfield is completely flat), and eventually to this big stone *castle* of a house. There, she met the woman whom she'd talked to on the phone, a sleek and stylish, thirtysomething-ish brunette named Marge Costner. Ms. Costner was so pleased with Annabel, she immediately said that if A.D. had any friends as serious as she was, they'd be welcome, too, "males as well as females."

The castle, which Ms. Costner told Annabel was a replica of a place called Frobisher Hall, in England, *did* have two small wings, and Annabel chose a nice room in the west one, which was otherwise unoccupied. The only slightly discomforting thing about her hostess and, indeed, the house, was the way the former talked about the latter, with respect to *sounds.* She said that Annabel might possibly hear noises in the night, but should ignore them. They were just, she said, the old place *settling,* which caused some wooden joists, or mortises and tenons, to rub up against some floorboards, or each other, making sounds that, in the darkness of the wee small hours, might possibly resemble *groans.*

Then, Tuesday night, I wrote another section, or chapter, of my opus, and this is how *it* went:

3

The thought of living in a groaning castle wasn't that disquieting to Annabel; she'd never been a scaredy-cat. Many things that frightened other girls (like spiders, boys with star-shaped silver studs along the fly front of their jeans, or Mrs. Crane the Latin teacher) didn't bother her at all. By nature, she was cool; she had also done karate class from ages ten through twelve. She decided that she'd try to analyze and understand the sounds the castle made; she'd try to think of them as "picturesque" and "atmospheric." But even she admitted that might take a little time, and could be better done with *company*.

At first, she thought that she might borrow Grace. The large brown dog looked like a fine companion, and she was pretty sure that Mrs. Costner wouldn't mind. But then she realized a dog, even such a bright and big and pleasant one as Grace, was not exactly perfect for the situation. Dogs don't crack jokes—and so relieve the tension of a "stakeout." Nor are they any good at formulating theories. No, she thought, she could do better.

"Heck," said Annabel D. Day, out loud, "what I ought to do is get a *person*—such as Martin Silverado."

The more she turned that over in her mind, the more it struck her as a wonderful idea. "Getting" Martin Silverado had occurred to her before, it just so happened, off and on, for years.

Although they'd started school together, kindergarten, twelve long years before, it's fair to say she didn't know him well. In certain ways, they weren't much alike. He was tall, long-headed and long-haired (he often pulled his black mane back, and wore it in a ponytail); she was on the short side, her face was sort of heart-shaped, and her auburn hair was naturally curly. Her home was stable and conservative; *his* parents both wore jeans and still would run to see the Grateful Dead, if they were ever anywhere within two hundred miles of Southport.

But where the two of them—herself and Martin Silverado—seemed to be alike was . . . well, in terms of basic *attitude*. They both were people who asked "Why?" a lot in class; the simple facts were not enough for them. And they both were disinclined to do what everybody else was doing; they liked to try new things. Sophomore year, he'd been allowed to meditate for phys ed credit—and when they'd studied the French Revolution in eleventh grade, *she'd* lived on cake and water for a week.

Because she knew these odds and ends concerning Martin Silverado, Annabel believed this castle deal might interest him. It didn't matter that he'd never acted interested in *her*. She decided she would seek him out, approach him.

"Martin! Hi!" she said, when she'd succeeded in so doing. He was perched on the big rock that protruded from the lawn in front of Southport High. Less mature members of the student body used it for games of King of the Hill. Martin Silverado was playing his tin whistle.

"Annabel D. Day! What's happening?" he asked. He rested his instrument on one well-muscled thigh.

"Not much," she said. "I really like that thing." She nodded toward the whistle. "But I was wondering. How'd you like to come and help me check out a phenomenon? It's in this sort of castle where I'm staying for a while. You could stay there, too. And it's free room and board."

"Whoa!" he said. "Jump back. Consider someone's interest *piqued*. Phenomenon, you say? A castle—and you're living there? With tapestries and gargoyles and *gonfalons*? Lay some further details on me, Lady Day. I beg of thee."

Annabel was pleased, though not surprised, by his reaction. She quickly told him how and where she'd read about this place that offered sanctuary, and how she'd gotten there, and all the things Marge Costner'd said to her concerning nighttime groans, and bringing friends to stay.

"The rooms are nice," she added, "and there's five or six that you can choose from." She stuck that in so that he wouldn't think that she was coming on to him, even if she semi, sorta, in-her-own-way was.

"Sounds like the ideal change of scene," he said, "and perfect timing, too. My parents and myself have more or less been getting on each other's nerves a little lately. They're good people—don't misunderstand—just, well, a little *immature*, at times."

Annabel assured him that she understood, and pretty soon they had it all decided. Martin would head home to "toss a few things in a sack," but he'd be at the castle "well before the dinner gong goes off."

"I look forward to real castle fare," he told her with that brilliant, white-toothed smile of his, "some roasted ox or haunch of venison. A few more meals at home and I'd have turned into a bean curd. That's what I told the lady mother, anyway."

Later on, when he arrived, he looked around and chose a room just down the hall from Annabel's. In fact, the only thing between his room and hers was an immense connecting bathroom, complete with a quite up-to-date Jacuzzi.

Hmm, thought Annabel as she considered all the *myriad* of possibilities that brought to mind. She frowned, but then remembered that there was a sliding latch that could prevent his entering the bathroom when she didn't want him to.

And also could be left unslid at other times, she thought; her frown became a smile.

I kind of liked that section, when I read what I had written. It seemed to me I'd rather neatly introduced some interesting elements: strange noises in the night (an old device, but still a grabber), *and* a slightly offbeat, but attractive, character. Ann Beattie–like, I didn't know along what lines this Martin Silverado–Annabel relationship would develop, but the situation, I believed (with them a bathroom's width apart), was *fraught* with life-enhancing possibilities.

And, in addition to all that, all these new developments were gen-u-wine, one hundred percent pure, fiction.

For about three days they were, in any case.

Allison moved into Kate Mycroft's place that Thursday, as she'd said she planned to do. I didn't rush right over there that night, or Friday either. My instincts told me it was best—not only best, but *right*—to let there be a space of private time in which my Allie and this Kate could start to get to know each other. By Saturday afternoon, however, all my writer's curiosities were crying out for satisfaction.

I'd gotten up quite late, for me, having gone on a movie date the night before with this boy I see more frequently than I really want to, Justin Sargent. It's sort of complicated. He's cute and smart enough, and in my Writing Workshop, but also pompous and . . . inept. When he gets around to doing what I guess he thinks is "making out," he does it pretty much as if it was a dangerous job—as if he's checking to make sure those things under my shirt *are* breasts, not mound-shaped, homemade bombs, affixed there by some terrorist. I keep telling myself I'm never going to go out with him again, and then I do. He's sort of a childish habit, like looking under the bed. And, too, my parents never ask me stuff about him. That's how absolutely harmless he appears to be. And is.

But anyway. I hung around the house until after eleven, Saturday morning, and then strolled down to Sycamore and up the drive to Mycroft House (as I now thought of it). I didn't even call ahead; there seemed no reason to. What could I be interrupting, after all?

When I got to the front door, I found it open, though a screen door blocked my way still. I pushed the bell, but got no answer. Then I knocked—to no avail. I put my face up close against the screen, and so could see right through the center hall and through another comparable screen door that opened on the patio, in back. And there, out there, was Allie, sitting at a table holding a croissant, and talking to somebody who I couldn't see. I opened the screen door and stepped into the hall. And as I did, I went, "*Yoo*-hoo!"

That got me recognition. Roger started barking, from the patio, where Allie was. I kept on going, crossed the hall, and reached the other door. Allie's head was turned toward me, and she was smiling. I opened the screen door and stepped out on the patio.

"Hi, Al. Hi, Roger. Hi, Kate . . ." I began, but stopped. I'd gotten one name wrong. "Hi, Malcolm," I concluded.

For sitting across the glass-topped table from Allison was not Kate Mycroft, but someone by the name of Malcolm Warren, another member of the junior class at Northfield High. He was, I couldn't help but notice, barefoot, and had on a tan cashmere sweater (V-necked, nothing under), and white shorts. His neatly combed brown hair looked wet, though not from any morning shower, it turned out. There were only clawfoot bathtubs in the servants' bathrooms (no Jacuzzis, either), and Malcolm had been there, in residence, since Friday morning.

"At dinner, Thursday night, Kate started in on all that 'fill the place with noise and laughter' stuff of hers, again," said Al, to me, by way of explanation. "So I called up Mal and asked him over, more or less to shut her up. He may be an idiot, but he's *sociable* enough, God knows."

Allie laughed, as she said that. She was also barefoot and had on a little number that I'd never seen before, a sort of Oriental-looking mini ("slut way up both sides," my mother might have said). Her and Malcolm's parents had always been best friends, but in spite of that the two of them had also got along, and even had gone together for a while the year before. Allie'd told me that had worked out pretty well, although at times it seemed like "borderline incestuous." I was pretty sure I'd never have that problem with him. Malcolm had a little Beamer and a completely carefree face. Why shouldn't he? I'd always thought. It wasn't *my* fault that we didn't know each other well. He always struck me as a gentleman, the kind of boy who knows his way around but doesn't advertise. The sort I'd like to have take up some pages in my . . . memoirs, assuming that I ever got a life worth writing about. But, of course, as long as Allie wanted him . . .

"Thanks a *lot,*" he said to Allie now. And, "Hi, Fleesh. It's good to see a friendly face. All she's been doing is abusing me. After getting me over here on false pretenses. I was expecting, like, a *house party*. Lots of noise and laughter all the time, *you* know." In spite of what he said, he didn't look like someone suffering, at all.

"Kate went downtown to get some stuff for a cookout tonight," Allison said to me. "You've got to join us, really. Bring anyone you want. Except your mother, maybe. Or just come by yourself. It really doesn't matter. Everything is really cool here. It'd be great if you could come and stay."

"Just don't bring *my* mother, either," Malcolm said. "She'd make us all play bridge, and I'm not kidding you. But Allie's right. It's really great here, Fleesh. You ought to come and stay. The more the merrier—and it'd make Kate happy. Too." He flashed a grin at me.

"Have some coffee," Allie said. "Sit down."

I went and got a cup, which gave me breathing space in which to process all this information I'd been getting, ever since I got there. First of all, here was life imitating art again. That made me mad; it *was* a pain. No sooner had I added Martin Silverado to my story than Allison brought Malcolm Warren into hers. And to further complicate the situation, I'd just gotten this peculiar—and completely unexpected—feeling that he might be getting interested in *me.* That had been a pleasant thing to think about before, but now that it was happening I found it mildly . . . petrifying.

While I drank my coffee, we talked about Kate and the house and how nice they both were. Malcolm and Allison were trying to decide whether to bring TVs from home or not; they both said this was an *ideal* place to do schoolwork, better than the library or anywhere. They were going to set up their PCs in the servants' dining room, they said, and jump right on their English term papers.

"Oh, and wait'll you hear this," Allie said to me. "There's even a *mystery* that goes with the house." She craned her neck to look back at the screen door and make sure there wasn't anybody coming. "We're pretty sure there's another person living here." She said that almost in a whisper.

"What?" I said. "How can there be? She showed us all the rooms on Sunday." I paused then, thinking back. "Didn't she?"

Allison hitched forward in her chair.

"That's just the point," she said. "She didn't. Don't you remember? I was telling Malcolm this exact same thing. There were a couple of closed doors, away down the hall, near her room, and she just sort of waved at them and said, 'More of the same,' or something like that. Meaning some more master bedrooms, I suppose, like the five or six she actually *did* show us. Don't you remember that?"

Now that she mentioned it, I did. And so I nodded.

"We're pretty sure that we've heard *voices,*" Allie said. "I mean another voice, talking to Kate. A deeper voice, a man's. It really didn't sound like TV or the radio; there's a difference, you can *tell.* And once she brought back a lunch tray from her room, supposedly, that had a lot more *stuff* on it—plates and cups and all—than one person'd use. We think that it's an invalid, maybe her father or someone like that. Someone *depressing,* that's Malcolm's theory. Which'd be why she wants some other people here, more or less as a distraction. Why she could use a little noise and laughter."

Malcolm was nodding, agreeing with himself, presumably.

"It's pretty logical," he said. "Allie told me she talked to you two about turning the house into a convalescent center, sometime? Now, what would have put *that* idea into her head? And what better place to keep a sick old man who didn't want to go into a nursing home, let's say. There has to be some reason that she bought this great ark of a house. I mean, a single woman in her *thirties*?"

I had to nod, myself. He had a point. Of course, if *I* was plotting the story, the mystery man wouldn't have been a sick father. He would have been a *lover,* who was (possibly) an artist, and reclusive—capable of sudden, monumental rages, in addition to great tenderness.

"Are you going to *do* anything?" I asked. "Try to find out more—check your theory out? Creep over there sometime when Kate's not here?" I smiled, and made my eyes mere slits, behind my spectacles. "Like *now*?"

The two of them exchanged a glance. That told me they'd discussed the possibility.

"I don't think so," Allie said, but not emphatically. "It isn't any of our business, really."

"And she's been so nice to us, and all," said Mal.

I couldn't disagree. Besides, the odds were pretty great they *weren't* right. Chances were, the two of them were overdramatizing and imagining. But—we writers *love* a mystery.

"Those voices—or that voice—did it, like, *groan*?" I inquired. "Could you make out any words? Anything at *all*?"

Five

I was careful not to overstay my welcome, at that point in time. But I did provide my friends sufficient opportunity to twist my arm a little more, and so agreed to come back for the cookout, later.

I walked home slowly, now savoring the odd relationship between the story I was working on and what was happening for real, at Mycroft House. By now, I felt that it had gone beyond coincidental to *bizarre,* the way the things I wrote about (made up, created) then actually took place, not five blocks from my home. Two more had been revealed to me this visit. I'd described how Annabel D. Day had brought a boy into the house that she was staying in; Allison, my friend, immediately did likewise. *I* wrote about strange sounds in Mrs. Costner's castle, sounds that Annabel and Martin were determined to investigate. And no sooner had I done so than Allison and Malcolm start describing noises that *they've* heard at Mycroft House, noises that they want to find out more about.

So, could I be blamed for thinking long and hard about just what I wanted to have happen next, in my novella, *Sanctuary*?

I hope that doesn't make you snort, or chuckle condescendingly. I suppose we writers tend to be a little more accepting than a lot of people are, when it comes to what I think is called "the paranormal"—things that can't be easily explained. I, myself, have been accused of being *credulous,* from time to time, although in other words. ("You eat up all this far-out crap you hear at school," is how my dainty mother puts it, "but just let someone like your father or myself . . ." *You* know.) It shouldn't be surprising, then, that what I decided to have happen next, in *Sanctuary,* was something that I might find . . . *pleasing* in real life.

The idea that I got, while walking home, was this: that I should add a character, somewhat like *me,* to my novella!

Instinctively, and all too ordinarily, I fear, I made my hands into a pair of fists and pumped them up and down, chest-high, in front of me. Oh, yes; I was excited. I had had a great idea, a flash, a message from the blue. One can't take credit for such windfalls, except in terms of receptivity. But a writer *should* maintain a constant state of readiness, I've always felt; one never knows exactly when one's muse may float some juicy bit in one's direction.

The name of my new character just popped up in my mind, no more than three steps farther down the street. She would be Fiona Garland (a lovely name, I think, don't you?), her first one being said "Fee-o-nah," just in case you've never heard of it. And she would have been a bosom bud of Annabel D. Day's ever since she'd moved to town, three years before.

"Fee" would also be creative—yes, in music. She would play, and write songs for, the oboe. This would allow her to walk around with a reed between her full, wet lips a lot (oboe players have to suck on their reeds to get them ready; I forget exactly why). And Fiona Garland would be very, *very* sexy. Not so much by reason of her looks (her physical endowments would be average), but more because of this amazing *air* she had. Men, of high-school age and older, took one look at her and saw their fondest dreams come true. They got the feeling that, with her (and here I hope I'm right about men's "fondest dreams"), they'd have one squarely on the fifty at the Super Bowl, a bottomless glass keg, that walnut gearshift knob screwed on a Lamborghini, and—most coveted of all!—the certain knowledge that they'd always do it perfectly, whatever "it" might be.

Annabel D. Day would know about the way that Fee affected males, of course. But still she wouldn't hesitate to ask her to the Costner castle. Martin Silverado would react to her, no doubt, but Fee would doubtless tell him to forget it. She was a loyal friend, and anyway, as Annabel well knew, she had her heart set (for the moment, anyway) on Lansing Pine, the banker's son, now halfway through his senior year at Yale.

When I got home, I went directly to my room and made some notes. It was tempting to haul out the manuscript and start to add to it at once. To get Fiona rooted in my story, and to have her start to . . . interact with Martin Silverado. I

mean, if life was going to keep on imitating art, why not let it get a move on?

But there were other things I also had to do, common-sense prerequisites, you *could* say. "Take a shower; wash your hair; smell good from head to toe"—my mother'd drilled those into me. I also did a little laundry and a speck of ironing. Being *in* a story laid some obligations on a girl, I told myself excitedly. And I'd promised to return to Mycroft House by half-past five.

It was probably five twenty-nine when I turned left off Sycamore and started walking up the drive to meet my destiny—as well as Allie, Kate, and Mmmm-alcolm Warren. Unlike many artists, I am very organized and punctual. A little *too* punctual, actually. I've had to make an effort to slow down, waste time, be less "right on the dot." So, now I get to places . . . oh, three minutes late. Exactly.

I'd probably got halfway up the drive when I began to hear an unexpected sound. It was coming from the woods ahead of me, and to my left. And it was heading toward the drive—a squeaky-wheel-type sound, it seemed to me.

I stood stock-still and waited. Pretty soon, I saw the source of it, between the trees: a wheelbarrow. Pushing it was someone who I didn't recognize, a boy about my age.

When he reached the blacktop, he saw me and stopped, and let the barrow down. I could see it had some big, flat stones in it; they must have been a heavy load.

"Hello," he said, but didn't smile. He also didn't have a shirt on, only boots and leather work gloves, and a pair of dirty jeans that had slid a good ways down his narrow hips. I couldn't call him "handsome," in that cool relaxing sense that Malcolm was. He had long blond hair, pulled back and gathered by a bright red rubber band—and a stud in his left ear. If he'd been in a band, he might have been the keyboard player, off to one side and only *interesting* looking—moody—his mouth a bit too small, his eyes too close together. He had absolutely *gorgeous* skin, though, smooth and honey-colored, with sufficient muscle underneath to make him more than "skinny."

"Hi," I said. I felt the need to say why I was there, to make it clear I wasn't trespassing. "I was invited here for dinner." I gestured, vaguely, toward the house. "I'm Felicia Gordon."

"Hello," he said again. "I'm . . . David. I'm Kate's gardener, and stuff. I do all the outside work, around the grounds." His eyes jumped here and there, as he said that. They hit my own a time or two, but didn't linger.

"Oh," I said, remembering. "I bet I saw you once before. Last Sunday. You were carrying some boards. That way." I used my thumb to show him where, in which direction. That seemed to me a cool and rather *flippant* thing to do. "You just work weekends here, or what?"

"No," he said. "I work any days I want. All seven of them, mostly. There's a lot to do." He didn't seem about to keep on going, with his load of stones. But neither did he seem . . . attracted. I figured he was enjoying the rest he was taking, although he'd never admit it.

"You don't go to Northfield High," I said, partly out of curiosity, partly to be saying something, anything. "At least, I've never seen you there."

"No," he said, and shook his head, with maybe just a little wispy smile. "Nope, I've kind of got an *allergy* to schools. . . ."

As he said that, he made some motions with his hands, sort of stirring up the air in front of him, so he could find the word he wanted in it. Watching him do that, I saw these marks on the insides of both his wrists, almost hidden by the tops of his gloves. They were lighter-colored lines across the skin (*striations?*), like some rows of narrow scars. Of course I thought: this boy once tried to slit his wrists—to kill himself.

"Well, do you live in town?" I asked. Now *I* was interested, and being nosy, but that's me. I claim that I can't help myself. Only Ms. Kevorkian insists I shouldn't try.

"I live right here," he said, and waved a hand in the direction he'd been going. "Kate's letting me camp out for now. I'm building her this sort of summer house; that's how come you saw me with that lumber. These rocks are for the terrace that I'm going to have in front of it, toward the brook." He took a real deep breath and let it out. "You want to come and look at it? It isn't really done yet."

This was strange. Now I had the feeling that he very much wanted me to see what he'd been doing. Ordinarily, I'd have thought twice before walking off into some strange woods with a half-naked boy I'd never met before, but this was not an ordinary deal, and my curiosity was on the bubble.

So: "Sure," I said. I looked down at my watch. "Provided that it isn't very far." That, I guess, was my concession to . . . normality.

"No," he said, "it's just a little ways." He lifted up the handles of the wheelbarrow and got it moving down the soft, brown path that headed to my right. "Thank God," he grunted back at me.

He told the truth; it wasn't far. I spent the little time it took admiring his back, but deciding that I didn't want to see much more of it. I *thought* the roundness of his butt would keep his pants up and it did, or *something* did. Before I figured any further, he had stopped and set the barrow down again.

"There," he said, unnecessarily.

"Gol-lee," I said. I couldn't help myself. "A *bower!*"

He turned and looked at me suspiciously, but that was what it sort of *was,* I think. What he'd made was like a little rustic shelter, related to a lean-to or a cabin, except open on three sides. The sloping roof was *thatched,* I guess you'd say, with hay and weeds and stuff, held more or less in place by pine boughs. In front of the shelter (which looked to be about the size of our living-room carpet, which I think is nine by twelve), there were a number of big flat stones, like the ones in the wheelbarrow. They weren't all the exact same thickness, and there were spaces in between them, so they sort of looked as much like stepping stones as like a terrace. A few feet beyond them was the brook.

"It isn't really finished," David said again. "I'd like to put a nice big hammock in it, for one thing. And I guess I've got to get some dirt, or sod, to put between those rocks. I found them in an old stone wall. Or maybe I should stick them in the ground somehow. I'm not exactly sure how people make a terrace."

"It'll be nice," I said. "This'll be a special place, when you get done."

I stepped up into the bower, not for any reason, just to be polite. There wasn't anything to see in there, but still I looked at everything: at the square posts that held up the four corners, and the smooth knotty boards that he'd used for the ceiling and the floor and the back wall. He wasn't a very good carpenter, I noticed. The boards were sawn unevenly, and you could see a bunch of hammer marks by

almost every nail head.

While I was going through this ritual, I had a sudden sense that I was being *scrutinized,* even to the point of "spied upon." I spun around, doing a graceful pirouette I hoped, and sure enough, this boy was staring at me, fixedly. He semi-smiled again, and looked away, looked sort of *smug*. I had the (stupid) feeling he had seen right through the jet-black long-sleeved polo I was wearing, and my flowered rayon skirt. That he now *also* knew that I had on a stretch lace bra, in black, and matching French bikini. I didn't think that he could see through *them,* I guess.

"How about that roof?" he said. "It was my idea, to put a thatched roof on. I always liked the way they look in pictures. The only trouble is, with mine the hay and crap kept blowing off. That's why I had to add the pine boughs. You think they look all right?"

"Oh, yes," I said, stepping out of the bower onto one of the stones, and looking up at the roof again. In fact, I thought it looked ridiculous, more like a compost heap than what you see in photographs of cottages in England. But David seemed to fish for compliments, and who was I to not gulp down the bait, way off there in the woods, alone, except for someone with his pants half off?

"The whole thing looks so . . . *atmospheric,*" I continued. "Everything fits in with every other element. I mean, it's perfect for the setting here."

"Yeah," he said. I wondered if he understood what I'd been saying. Boys sometimes seem a little . . . *"duh"* (if you know what I mean), if you say anything more subtle than "I really like your sweater (car, the way you kiss)."

I took another quick look at my watch.

"Oh, boy," I said. "I'm late; I've got to run. So, thank you for the *tour,* and good luck with the terrace. . . ." I was facing him, but also walking up the path, away from him. "I'll see you."

"Right. So long," he said. He picked a stone up, out of the wheelbarrow. His body language wasn't hard to understand: "Not interested in you." But of course he'd acted that way all along, except for that one stare I'd caught him giving me.

His attitude was fine with me. He reminded me of cats I'd known. Bodies beautiful, but lacking any warmth or personality.

I hustled toward the house, now *really* late; my watch said twenty-two of six, already.

The cookout was a lot of fun. Kate had one of those big black spherical grills that look like part of an astronomy unit, and she'd parked it by the patio. Malcolm volunteered to start the charcoal fire and even cook the steaks that Kate had bought, provided I would share the responsibility for deciding when they were done.

"I hate to cut-and-peek," he said. "That's really bush. My father sort of *feels* them with the back of the fork; he won't even jab and test for juiciness. Actually, it's kind of gross, to watch him—too much touchy-feely. But I have to give him credit. His steaks are always perfect."

"Gee," said Allison. "Just think. You're going to inherit money, and you can wash a car already, right? So, if you learn to cook a steak like Dad, you'll be all set. What else does any husband have to know?" She grunted. "Just you two tell me when you *think* they're almost ready, and I'll bring my great potato salad out. Now *there's* a work of culinary art." She looked at me and winked. "Of course it's Thalia's recipe."

I'd mentioned meeting David to Kate, when I first got there. She was home to hear me knocking on the front screen door this time. I made him my excuse for being late, which was the simple truth, except I wasn't really late at all. Malcolm and Allison were both still upstairs getting dressed, or taking baths, or making out for all I knew, except that Allie'd said she doubted that she ever *really* would, with him.

Kate acted a little surprised that I'd met her groundskeeper, still working at that time of day, and she asked me something that I remember thinking was a little strange.

"How did he seem?" she said. We were standing in the big front hall.

"All right," I said, not knowing what she meant, exactly. Pleasant? Irresistible? Completely stoned? Peculiar? I thought of the scars I'd seen on both his wrists. "He's pretty quiet. But he seemed to take a lot of pride in . . . well, his work. That little house he's building for you."

"Good," she said. "That's good." She turned and started toward the kitchen. "I thought it might be nice to cut up strawberries and peaches and have them with vanilla ice cream for dessert. D'you suppose that you . . ."

So, moments later, I was busy with a paring knife and David, as a subject, was kaput. As my father likes to say these days, "No problem."

During dinner, I watched Al and Mal do one fantastic job of conversation-steering. I was sure they must have made some plans, worked out a strategy ahead of time, upstairs.

Allie started the ball rolling when she said how much her grandmother enjoyed Thalia's potato salad. Apparently, Granny claimed that it was far superior to the one served at the blue-ribbon retirement community, where she presently resided.

Then Malcolm said *his* parents always swore great oaths that they would never go into *any* old person's setup, be it a "senior village," or a nursing home, or whatever.

Allie said her parents weren't that extreme, maybe because her grandmother was basically so happy where *she* was, but that her father kept telling her sister, Riley, and herself (kiddingly, she thought) that he expected them to *personally* take care of him, in their own homes, someday, just as he had taken care of them, in his.

After a certain point, it seemed as if Kate or I would have to say something about *our* parents and this issue and, sure enough, she did. She said her parents had sold the business they'd been in, a year or two before, and had bought a house in Scottsdale, Arizona, where they'd made a million friends and absolutely loved it.

"My father plays his eighteen holes a day, year round, which gets him out from under Mother's feet," she said. "His energy level is disgusting. He'd carry his own clubs if they allowed it; he hates it that they make him use a cart. Usually, he swims a bunch of laps when he's through golfing. Daddy's always stayed in shape. They owned the biggest chain of fitness centers in the world, and he practiced what he preached. So did Mom and I, for that matter—being typically compliant females." And she made a face. "My parents still seem young; they're only sixty-two."

I watched while Allison and Malcolm looked at each other after she'd said that. So much for their solution to the Mystery at Mycroft House—the voice they thought they'd heard, those extra dishes. I didn't know about the two of them, but I was sure Kate wasn't lying; I can tell. We writers are good liars; looked at in a certain light, that's what fiction is, a pack of lies. So, being one, I'd know one, wouldn't I?

After dinner, we all washed and dried and put away the plates and bowls and silverware and glasses that we'd used. Amazingly enough, even doing that was fun, with everybody pitching in and kidding back and forth, and no one acting like the boss, or martyred.

"You know, you ought to come and live here, too," Allie said to me. "Even if there wasn't any other reason, we could use your basic household skills. Your mother's trained you well, m'dear."

"I'd love it if you could," said Kate. "You saw there's loads of room. And, well, you seem like part of this already."

"Yeah, come on, Fleesh," Malcolm said. "Can't you see we want you, *need* you, have to *have* you—*bay*-bay." And he put a sort of comic grab on me, and bent me over backward (yes, as if to kiss me) in the manner of a Musketeer, or Cyrano, or Rudolph Valentino. I went along with it, and as his lips brushed by my ear, he whispered, "Please, please, *please*."

"I'll have to see," I said when I was vertical again. "You know I'd like to, you-all. But, well, my mother is the problem, as Allison well knows. Maybe if she talked to you," I said to Kate.

"By all means have her call me," she replied. "I could tell her it'd be a kindness to dear Allie here, as well as a big help to *me*." She smiled. "All of which is true."

I nodded and smiled back at her. I didn't have a thing to

lose, and possibly a lot to gain. When we were through in the kitchen, we all played a couple of games of that old board game Sorry. After that, Malcolm and Allie and I made popcorn and sat around and gossiped. It was all good wholesome fun; the three of us were getting real relaxed with one another.

Of course, I'd been relaxed with Allison *forever,* and that doubtless made it easier for me not to be overawed by Malcolm and his . . . pedigree. The word on Mr. Warren, Malcolm's father, is that he doesn't have to work at all; the family has old, old money. But work he does, though maybe not that hard. He owns the *Northfield Record*—that's the local paper. It comes out three times a week and, according to my dad, it loses money every year, but not a lot of money. Before his father bought the *Record* for him, Mr. Warren learned the newspaper business by working at the *San Francisco Examiner* for three years. I know that because he often drops the clause "as we used to say at the *Examiner*" into the column that he writes for the *Record,* called "Chumming." I've always thought the column was as precious as its name.

But, be that as it may, Allie drove me back to my place after midnight. My mother was awake, as usual, and called "Good night" to me as I went by their door. Only after I had gotten into bed did I remember David, and the fact that I hadn't even mentioned him to Al and Mal. That hadn't been on purpose; my mind had been too full of other things. I'd tell them all about him up at school on Monday, at the latest. And then I had another thought: Could David actually be *living* in the house, never mind that "camping" story? Could it have been *his* voice that Mal and Al had heard? Possible, it seemed to me. *Plausible* enough—but likely? I'd bring that question up with Al and Mal, as well.

Just before I went to sleep, I thought I'd have to write a scene in which Fiona Garland's mom agrees that it'd be a great idea to have her daughter move right into Costner's Castle. Smiling over that one, I dozed off.

Six

The next day, being Sunday, I had time. Time to do my stuff, take care of business, be myself. I think I'm much more like *Felicia Gordon* when I'm home, in my own room. At school, I always feel I'm acting like a used-car salesman, only kicking my own tires.

This Sunday, I decided I'd skip church. I told my mother I had too much schoolwork that I had to do. She nodded, looking smug. I'm sure what she was thinking was: Felicia's growing up; she's picking up on an important truth, that there isn't *time* to go to church on Sunday (or on any other day); that adults have to be responsible, put first things first. And then my mother took a sponge and started rubbing the refrigerator.

Safely in my room, I started working on my book, on Chapter Four, beginning with a conversation between Annabel D. Day and her friend Fiona Garland. I had Annabel positively bubbling over with enthusiasm about life at Costner's Castle, and then with excitement over how she and Martin Silverado *both* heard distant sounds the night before that seemed to them more human than, say, architectural. And, as they talked, Annabel began to focus on how nice it'd be to have Fiona living there, too. Fee, for her part, saw that the castle'd be a *great* place to practice the oboe, far away from anyone it might disturb. She mentioned that, and Annabel was pleased to realize her friend would surely choose a room way down the wing from hers and Martin Silverado's—even on a different *floor,* most likely.

And that, in fact, is what Fiona did. But first she sold her mother on the move by getting her to see how *helpful* someone like Marge Costner could turn out to be, to a musician getting started. Mrs. Garland, who had seen the movie *Amadeus,* knew therefore that fortunate composers and performers (such as Mozart) all had wealthy "patrons" who supported them and got them started on the road to great success. And so she easily could see—admit—that in *this* day and age a patron might—just might—pick up the tab for college.

(I even had her mother lend Fiona a scarf of hers, one that she knew Fiona liked, and, after, help her load stuff in the car.)

Once settled in the castle (and now in Chapter Five), Fee

joined Marge and Annabel and Martin for a typically exotic gourmet meal in the huge banquet hall: lamb kidneys sautéed in a red wine and herb sauce, served on a bed of wild, wild rice and arugula leaves. (It turned out that Mrs. Costner was the author of some seven witty, worldly cookbooks, and was currently at work on number eight, entitled *Fiddling with Organ Pieces; Recipes from the Innard Sanctum.*) After dinner, the three kids and Grace, the big brown dog, watched television on the enormous set in the Great Hall, Annabel and Martin more or less reclining on a sofa, Fee in her own chair, her eyes fixed firmly on the lighted screen, with Grace down by her feet. By midnight, they were all ready for bed, but they agreed to reconvene two hours later, in A.D.'s room, there to see if they heard any groaning sounds that night, together.

From that point, I moved directly on to Chapter Six, which went as follows:

6

When Fee's alarm went off, at ten to two, it seemed to her she'd only been asleep five minutes. But she struggled to her feet, pulled on a pair of pants and a big T-shirt (she'd gone to bed in just a little bra-seamed camisole and "no-know" thong bikini), jabbed her feet into her favorite pair of clogs, stuck an oboe reed between her glistening red lips, and headed for the door.

But, before she got to it, she remembered that the castle's halls were all unlighted, so she struck a match and fired up the candle in the nice brass holder by her bed. *Then* she opened up her door and started down the long dark hall, heading for the stairs.

When she reached her friend's room minutes later, she found out that Martin was already there. Or, possibly, "still there." Annabel D. Day, Fiona knew, had come and gone for years, just as she pleased. And from what she'd said to Fee, she'd gone a good ways, more than once, on pretty far-out streets (as well as speedy super-highways), and with less attractive boys (Fee thought) than the black-maned Martin Silverado.

Also in the room, and getting to her feet as Fee came in, was Grace, the dog, who also smiled at her, and wagged her tail, as usual. It seemed already clear that Grace was purely overjoyed that she and Annabel had come to Costner's Castle. Whenever she was able to, she scratched (discreetly) at their doors. Now Fiona patted her, and called her "sweetie-pie."

Martin, not to be outdone by charming canines, jumped up, too, and offered Fee high fives. Surprised, she slapped his hands right back (but didn't pat the guy or call him names), at that point unsuspiciously. He was barefoot, and he now had on a pure white Mexican wedding shirt and what looked like maroon pajama bottoms, smooth-as-satin ones. He also had a big idea.

"What we oughta do," he said, "is all three chill out on the bed here, side by side. That'll put us in the self-same, sympathetic a-u-aural zone, you know? And then we douse the lights, like every one of 'em."

"Okay, cool," said Annabel D. Day. She sat down on the bed and patted the space right next to her. Martin, who'd been thinking more along the lines of *horizontal*, decided not to press the point. He sat; Fiona took her place beside him. She blew her candle out, and Annabel switched off the bedside lamp.

It was completely quiet in the room, and very, very dark. Time passed; Fiona started feeling sleepy. But, seconds later, she came wide awake. There was something pressing up against her ankle, gently rubbing it. It could have been the dog, except it wasn't hairy. It might have been a snake, except it felt quite warm.

Fiona moved her foot away, broke contact with . . . the item. But, a moment later, contact re-occurred. She moved her foot again, then lifted it and brought it down, heel first, not fast but hard, and with a grinding motion. Remember, she was wearing clogs.

"Ah-ooga-hooga-hooga," Martin Silverado went, his cry of pain transformed, almost at once, into a fit of coughing.

"Sorry. Little accident," he whispered—quite equivocally, Fiona thought when he had stopped.

"Hey—everybody makes mistakes," replied Fiona sweetly, also in a whisper.

It wasn't too much later that the groans began, or anyway some sounds that seemed a lot like groans. But they came from far away, way far away. No one could say for sure who/what was making them, if they were animal, or vegetable, or (even) mineral in origin. The three of them all listened hard—assiduously, in fact—but still could not determine what it was, exactly, they were hearing.

"Let's try to find out where it's coming from," said Annabel D. Day, enthusiastically. She turned the bedside lamp on. Fee and Martin blinked and nodded; he had a red mark on the instep of one foot. The dog blinked also, yawned, and fell asleep again.

Fiona got her candle lit again; all of them except for Grace then stealthily slid out the door into the corridor and started walking down it toward the center of the castle. They reached the Great Hall and passed through it, entered the east wing. The sounds were clearer there; it seemed that they were coming from the second floor.

Fiona, who had close to perfect pitch, had no idea what she was hearing—but she knew it wasn't music. Martin, who had spent his childhood living in a commune, thought the groans had more to do with *effort* than with pain. Annabel D. Day, like many very pretty girls, was not disposed to speculate too much, and just enjoyed the . . . well, *excitement*, which she found that she was feeling.

They'd climbed the big stone staircase and had reached the second floor when, unexpectedly, the noises stopped.

"Quick," said Martin Silverado in a whisper. "Kill the flame." Fiona blew her candle out.

When their eyes had grown accustomed to the darkness in the hall, they could tell that lamps were on in two rooms on the corridor; from underneath two doors there came a shaft of light. One lighted room was on their right, and fairly close to where they were; the other, on their left, was maybe halfway down the corridor.

The trio stood there, still as statues, uncertain as to what to do. And suddenly, the nearer light blinked off; the door to that room opened, and a someone who they couldn't see stepped out into the hall. To their great relief, she/he began to slowly navigate the nearly pitch-black corridor, heading in the opposite direction.

A surprisingly familiar smell came wafting toward the nostrils of the three adventurers, the odor of the art room back at Southport High. Just as they began to process that surprising fact, the other person in the hallway reached his destination (his *or* hers). The door way down there on the left swung inward, fast, and was followed by a slight, robed figure, who then closed the door again, you *could* say slammed it, even. The watchers never had a chance to see if he or she was male or female, dark or light, close to their own age or boring, adorable or scuzzy.

"Let's get our heinies out of here," said Annabel D. Day in a tiny but emphatic whisper. She started moving hers toward the staircase, even as she spoke, one hand against the wall, in nearly total darkness.

Fiona started after her, but then remembered she had matches in her pocket and a candle in her hand. What the heck, she thought, and stopped, and fished the matches out.

Martin Silverado, accidentally or on purpose, collided with the motionless Fiona's shoulder, and possibly to keep himself or her from falling, wrapped his arms around the rest of her. She, spun partway by the collision, found herself pressed up against him, front to front. She had to give him credit: he felt good, smelled good. What she didn't realize was that Martin, thinking much the same about the way *she* felt and smelled, decided he would try to kiss her. And so he did his best to aim his partly opened, firm-lipped mouth at hers.

What he'd forgotten—who could blame him?—was: Fiona had an oboe reed gripped loosely in her teeth. And because his aim was just a little off—not too surprising in the dark—before his mouth got to her face at all, he found he had a reed-end up his nose.

''Geetch,'' he muttered, wincing in surprise and minor pain, and letting go of the girl.

''What?'' said Annabel D. Day, quite understandably confused.

''Nothing, really,'' said Fiona, as she finally struck a match. Once she got the candle going, they were able to return to A.D.'s room quite quickly, there to start to sort out all they'd seen and smelled and heard.

When I was finished writing and rereading all of that—three chapters' worth of work—I heaved a weary sigh. "Weary" 'cause it was, had been, a lot of hard, hard work. Writing isn't something that you just toss off, tra-la-la, what fun; there's a lot of heavy lifting in it, even when you've practiced for a while. And a "sigh" because I felt I might be compromising the integrity, indeed the worth, of my novella as a piece of fiction, in order to promote my selfish ends (or even my "libidinous ambitions," you could say). I'd shoved this girl Fiona right into a plot that didn't really need her, and then I'd made this Martin Silverado, Mr. Sexy, start hitting on the kid. Had I sold out literature by doing so? Or could I argue that, in this one case at least, the ends would justify the means? After all, the thing I thought to be at stake was my—Felicia Gordon's—*growth,* her depth and breadth of understanding of the world of men and women. She would never write with wit and wisdom—or with sympathy and empathy—until she knew, had tasted, life a lot more . . . heartily, whole-heartedly, than she had done to date.

So, I told myself, I had to do what I was doing. And with that I *hied* myself downstairs to find my mother.

I found her—oh, surprise, surprise—still (?) in the kitchen. She'd (obviously) just washed the floor, because not only were the kitchen table and four chairs now sitting in the sitting room, but also the refrigerator and the stove were still pulled away from the wall. My mother is the only person I know who washes the floor under the refrigerator and the stove no less than twice a month—a rarity in itself—and also, devotionally, waxes it. I sometimes wonder who she's trying to impress—the cockroaches? But of course there aren't any cockroaches. My mother doesn't share our living space with any other living, eating squashables.

"Ah, just in time," I said, and flipped face forward to my knees and hands, as if I'd finally made my choice of faith, and it was Islam.

Or, if not Islam, the gospel according to St. Mom. "There's no ladylike way to clean a kitchen or a bathroom floor," she's told me many times, down through the years.

Knee to knee, and sometimes cheek by jowl, we rubbed that wax into the surface of those imitation tiles, and as we worked, we talked—of different waxes and floor coverings, of back-and-forth compared to circular, and finally of Mycroft House, and how I'd been invited to stay over there awhile.

My sales kit had three items in it. One, I could keep a valued friend from feeling strange and lonely. Two, I could help out Mrs. Mycroft with the housework (something Allie wasn't great at). Doing so would (three) endear me to a person who had gone to Vassar, one of my first choices, and whose good opinion, tucked inside my folder there, might move it to the "must take" pile.

"It seems to me I've had a golden opportunity fall right into my lap," I said. "It'd mean a lot of extra work for me, my going over there, but, well, it seems like something I should *do*. What do *you* think, Mom?"

"Well, I suppose that it'd be all right," she said. "You wouldn't be that far away, in case you hated it. Maybe I'll call up this Mrs. Mycroft, and the two of us could have a little chat."

Elation blossomed in my bosom, but I kept on rubbing, solemnly—which is the way a person cleans (I'd known for years). You see, I also know my mother, so I knew that last line was a test. If I said no, she shouldn't call up Mrs. Mycroft, she would be suspicious, think that there was something I was trying to hide from her. And if I jumped for joy at the idea, she'd smell another kind of rat, and think that she was missing something. So:

"Well, I guess you *could* do that" I grunted, laying on the *elbow grease,* safely on the middle ground. "The whole thing's up to you and her." They were the Major Powers, I was saying—I, a tiny Third World country. "I guess she wouldn't mind. Just please don't mention *Vassar,* will you? We wouldn't want her thinking we were trying to *use* her, would we?"

My mother nodded, then she shook her head. She could play the diplomat, do this *and* that, be devious. She really could. The two of them would have a lovely chat, I knew, and Mom would let me go. The kitchen floor had done its part; it glistened and it glowed. We were a partnership, we Gordon women. Say what you will about my mom (and, as you know, I do), she only wants what's best for me, the same as I do.

It took me almost half the day at school before I got some time alone with Al and Mal. I'd been holding in my news so long, I fear my eyes were bugging out.

"Guess what?" is how I started telling, I'm ashamed to say. At least I didn't make them guess. "I'm in! My mom *did* call up Kate, and everything's all set. I'm moving in tonight."

"Fan*tas*tic," they both said. Their faces said the same, but differently, I thought. For Allie, this was news she'd thought she'd be receiving. Whatever Allie wants, Allie gets—that kind of thing. Not that she wasn't really pleased, for both of us. It's just that Allison expected things to work out right for her in life. Maybe that was part of being rich, or being beautiful, I wouldn't know. I was pretty sure it wasn't merely being unimaginative.

But Malcolm lighted up in more of a little-kid-on-Christmas-morning kind of way. At least it seemed to me he did; of course, that *could* be wishful thinking. You know that romance magazine expression: "Something unspoken passed between them"? (My mother leaves such magazines around the house sometimes, like in the bathroom; that's how *I* just *happened,* once, to read it.) Well, that's sort of what occurred in this case. And the unspoken something could have been this single word: "A*ha*!"

(I've got to be half right; I know what I was trying to "pass.")

After that, I filled them in on David, describing him and what his role was on the Mycroft property, and asking both of them if they had ever known a kid who looked like that, either there at school or just in town.

They both said no, they didn't, and Allie said, "But did you *like* him? Did you think he's *cute*?" She made a teasing face at Mal.

"Not cute," I said. "Lots too reptilian to be cute, and maybe not the smartest kid in camp. I don't think he'd be my type, exactly," I said casually, as if I had a type.

"Actually, I met him yesterday, myself," said Allie. Malcolm looked surprised; she'd waited long enough to say.

"Remember, after lunch?" she said to him. "When I asked you if you wanted to walk down to the drugstore, and you said no, you were going to work on your *paper*? Then. He was trying to make a dam in the brook, and he was really botching up the job. He had on this tiny little pair of swimming trunks, like the kind they wear in the Olympics, only his were sort of a Hawaiian print. I felt like telling him to put a pair of boxers on, or *jams,* or something." Allie made a gesture that I'd seen her make a hundred times before. David was of little interest; David was dismissed.

This wasn't snobbery, though it may sound like that. Allie kissed off people from all walks of life, for many sorts of reasons. But not because a person was *beneath* her, on some social scale. It seemed as if either she was a fan of someone's or she didn't deal with him or her at all.

I asked her, though, if she thought maybe David was the voice they'd heard, if maybe *he* was staying in the house. She said she really doubted it, but anything was possible, she guessed—although it didn't seem he'd be Kate's type. It looked as if she simply wasn't interested in David—and that Malcolm wasn't, either.

What *he* seemed to want to know some more about was my arrival at the house. When, exactly, would I get there, did I think? And so on. And as we went our separate ways to different classes, he contrived to touch me. Not as . . . *pushily* as Martin Silverado might have. It was almost what you'd call a *pat,* just on the shoulder, sort of, with a little *stroke* in it, as well. And accompanied by both his *very* white-toothed smile and eye contact, unlimited.

He did have lovely, *honest,* hazel eyes, set nice and far apart, it seemed to me.

Seven

My mother drove me over to the Mycroft house—surprise, surprise. She'd never miss a chance to check the sanitary standards in another woman's house, *and* meet the person who was going to be her surrogate (job description: keeping daughter's virtue, as they say, "intact") for the next three weeks or so.

The visit went quite well, I thought; my virtue never even got discussed. Kate charmed my mother into coffee and dessert, and told her that this summer she was going to get her hair cut just like Mom's. Allie also positively *oozed* good fellowship, showing Mom her room and helping me (or her, or us) decide to take the light and airy one a little down the hall from hers. It overlooked the grounds behind the house: the tennis court, this big square maze they had, the formal gardens, and the pool.

Malcolm made a contribution, too; he stayed completely out of sight till Mom was gone. Earlier, he'd locked away all telltale signs that there was someone male in residence— such things as baseball cards and brass spitoons, girlie magazines and jock straps.

We got into a great routine at once, I thought; it wasn't anything like home, at Mycroft House. First of all, the three of us would get up on our own, and eat, and leave for school before Kate even came downstairs. As a rule, we had the time to walk, though Allie's 'stang was there for backup, or in case of rain. Because our schedules were different, we'd head for "home" at different times. And, much as I liked school, I got to feeling that I couldn't wait.

What we decided was, we'd divvy up the chores by having "teams" (of two), each of which would cook and do the cleaning up on one night, and then be waited on the next. Inasmuch as Kate and I were more "experienced," we were made the "captains" of the teams. Then Kate wrote down the other two names on slips of paper, which she folded up and put inside a colander ("that thing with all the holes," to Malcolm). She also claimed first pick, "seeing as we're in my house," and that way she chose Allison.

"Hooray," said Kate. "A franchise player. Prepare for a potato salad every other night."

"Poor Fleesh," said Mal and Al, almost together.

But me, I flashed my good sport's smile, and imagined teaching him the proper way to toss a big green salad, standing sort of like a golf pro, with my arms around him, from behind.

After dinner, when the dishwasher was loaded and humming away, we gravitated to the spacious "game room," starting on the first night I was there. This was also Kate's idea—that it made a lot of sense to start our food digesting with a little passive exercise, in the form of skittles, darts, or billiards (three team sports I'd never played before). Then, she said, we'd study better, after, as a consequence. I don't know if she was right or not, but this "gaming period," as Allison named it, soon became a high point in our day. We did a lot of what my father calls "horsing around," trying to take unfair advantage of one another (cheating), and getting pretty physical in our attempts to throw opponents out of synch. There surely was a lot of noise (like shrieks and groans) and laughter in the house, when we were playing games. I was pleased to feel that Kate—who was just as giddy as the rest of us—was (also) getting some returns on her investment.

When the games were over, Malcolm, Allison, and I *did* hit the books, either in our rooms or in the former servants' dining room, our study hall. Because we all took different classes, we worked different hours; I was often last to leave the study hall, and Allie—the original Ms. Speedy—was often first. But—each by his or her own standard—all of us worked pretty hard, I think. I know that I had things to prove, not only to my mother, but also to myself: that I could handle being on my own, the way I would be when I got to college.

One strange thing was: The first six days that I was there,

neither Allie, Mal, or I heard any voices, footsteps, groans, or other sounds suggesting that there was someone else residing in the house. Nor did we see a single empty pizza box or dirty plate that couldn't be accounted for. It seemed that with my getting there the other person—if there ever was one—just took off, or something. "Nice going, Fleesh," said Allie when the subject came up once. "It probably was just Keanu-baby-doll, or Kiefer."

My room, as I implied, was nearer Allison's than Malcolm's, and having her so close, so constantly, was great. Growing up, it had just been me and Michael, and he was always in a different world from me. In Mycroft House, right from the start, Allie seemed a lot the way I thought a sister would be. We shared a bathroom, even borrowed antiperspirants and socks, and wandered in and out of each other's rooms, and gabbed and gabbed and gabbed. She ran occasional "errands" in her car—going up to her parents' house to water the plants or get something—but mostly we hung out. I felt like asking her to tell me where things stood with her and Malcolm, but I didn't dare. I was afraid she might say she had overcome her qualms and now had started up a second "gaming period," this one in his room, and late at night.

The fourth day I was there, on Thursday afternoon, I had another—what? encounter?—with that David person. I was coming back from school and walking up the driveway, by myself, when I saw a bicycle, a ten-speed, quite a lean and hungry-looking one, propped up against a tree. I supposed that it was Malcolm's, but I couldn't guess what it was doing there.

"Good afternoon, Felicia."

The voice, mock-solemn and pitched extra-deep, boomed down on me from up the tree the bike was leaning on. It made not just my heart but all the other organ pieces in my chest take quite a jump, although I like to think my feet stayed on the ground.

He was sitting on a limb, not way way up, with both legs dangling. He had no helmet on, but otherwise was dressed like all those slender men—a lot of them with beards—you see on bikes on weekend mornings, pedaling like mad along less-traveled country roads. In other words, he wore a short-sleeved top and shorts made out of very smooth elastic stuff, material the wind would slip right off, while it (the suit) kept clinging to the wearer's body parts.

"Oh, hi," I said. "So, how's the weather up there?" I was still a little jumpy, but there's no excusing lines like that from someone who . . . *you* know.

"Fine, fine," he said. "It's fun to look at people sometimes when they think they're unobserved. Although this time I had the bike down there, and so you weren't off your guard, I guess." He paused. "I knew you'd be the next one by."

I decided I'd just let that pass. "What about the summer house?" I said. "And terrace? I've been wondering." A total lie, but I've admitted I'm a liar.

"I'm done with it," he said. "That stupid thing. There's lots of other stuff to do."

Unlike the last time, he didn't seem to want to show, as well as tell.

"You having dinner here again?" he asked, but looking off into the distance, underlining his indifference to my answer—and the rest of me.

"No, actually I'm living here," I said. "Kate invited me. I moved in Monday night."

"I know," he said. I thought he was the kind who'd *always* know. "You want to play some tennis sometime?"

"Gee," I said, "I'm really not a tennis player." That was true. Although I'd always thought I'd like to be one—but below the level where you're grunting all the time. "I'm also pretty busy nowadays." I waved a hand around and fed him one of his old lines. "There's a lot to do."

"I can teach you; it's a simple game," he said. And with that he pushed himself right off the limb and dropped down to the ground. He landed lightly, with his knees bent, and he needed only one step forward to regain his balance.

"So, how many of you *are* there now?" he said.

"Still one," I said, holding up one finger, making it pop up and down. "I'm totally non-schiz." Of course I knew what he was asking, but I felt like being . . . "smart."

"I meant living at the house," he said. He wheeled the bike onto the driveway, heading out, away.

"Well . . ." I took my time, intentionally. "Let's see. There's Kate and . . . one, two, three of us. And we really are enjoying being here."

"How nice," he said. "A gleesome threesome." And he gave the bike a push, got on, and started pedaling away without another word. I turned to watch him go. He accelerated fast, his body bent way over, flattened out above the handlebars, his butt raised up a little, off the seat. In no time, he was out of sight.

Just for the heck of it, I took the path he'd led me down before. As I approached the little house, I saw its "terrace" hadn't changed from when I'd seen it last; it was still a bunch of big flat stones, just scattered on the ground. In fact, the only change that I could see was an addition to the . . . *decor* (?) of the house. Now, inside, there was a mattress on the floor that had at least one rumpled sheet on it. No hammock still, but certainly a full- (or queen-?) sized mattress, quite a comfy-looking one.

My mother's genes kicked in. This kid is being *paid*? (I thought.) For camping out and doing crummy work and being weird to guests? He was the one . . . *accessory* at Mycroft House that didn't seem to fit. I wondered if his bike was stolen—it *did* fit.

I made a mental note to pose some subtle questions to our hostess; there must be more to this than met the eye. Why did she tolerate this kid? Not that I really cared. It was just my curiosity, kicking in again.

Friday, Mal and I served up a dish my mother thinks is "very snazzy"; its name—and I'm translating from the French—is Chicken Veronica. She found the recipe in a cookbook that my brother gave her, called *The Sixty-Minute Gourmet*. It calls for seedless grapes in the sauce—Mom uses red ones—and she loves to make it for relatives of ours, and other connoisseurs of *haute cuisine,* and watch them try to figure out (before they put them in their mouths) just what in hell those red things are.

"This is considered a real delicacy in the south of France," she likes to say at that point in the meal. "They call it Chicken Veronica because they found that Chicken 'n Eyeballs turns some people off." Right after that, of course, she tells them what the red things really are, but there is still a lot left over, always.

We couldn't pull that gag, not on Allison and Kate; they were two sophisticated eaters, who of course had had the dish before, and loved it. After dinner, Allie had to go up home, to do the plants and make a bunch of phone calls ("mainly to my parents"), while Kate was heading to a movie, one that Mal and I had seen before and that, in fact, I'd recommended to her. All of which meant he and I were left alone to do our cleaning up, and then . . . play games, one on a side, or something. Because it was Friday, there were parties we could go to, but. . . . We had the estate, all to ourselves.

When we'd flicked the Maytag on, his lordship looked at me and said, "What say, instead of throwing darts, we take a stroll around the grounds, m'deah?" He curled the tip end of a most imaginary mustache. "Go watch the silver moon reflecting off the pool, and all that rot?"

What could I do but curtsy and say, "Sounds like fun"? A lot of things, I guess, but my creative tendencies were being overawed by other . . . urges. And so, off we strolled.

He took my hand almost at once. His was big and warm and . . . *confident,* I thought; there wasn't any of the stress that went along with holding some boys' hands—Justin Sargent's, for example. If Malcolm were to go from holding hands to something else, he'd make (I felt quite sure) a smooth *transition,* so whatever he (or we) did next, it would merely seem to be completely natural, and logical, and *welcome*. Hmm, I thought; good writing and successful making out may have some things in common. How *serendipitous,* I thought. We kept on strolling and, indeed, soon came upon the pool, and stood there, looking down at it.

"Isn't it amazing," Malcolm said, "how we've gone from being almost total strangers to good friends in . . . what? Five days or something?"

"I know," I said. "It is. I've been thinking the same thing. What do you suppose it is? This place? The special situation?" Of course I didn't say, or even think, "This book I'm writing?" Not while this was going on. Life and literature were, for the moment, very separate entities.

"Another weird part is," he said, "this all seems so completely natural." He squeezed my hand a little. "It's like everyone fits in with everybody else, and with the *house,* and all. I almost get the feeling this was something we were meant to do."

I wondered what I'd do if he suggested skinny-dipping then. Just as another something "natural" that we were "meant to do"? I'd never done that in my life, not with a boy at least, and yes, the moon was very bright. I thought: Should I look at my watch and see how long it was since we'd had dinner? And then I thought: Would Alice Walker have a thought like that?

But before I'd even answered those ("No" and "No" are right, of course), we'd started strolling once again, around the pool and past some garden plots, heading toward the maze. It loomed up darkly in the bright moonlight.

I guess you know what mazes are, in general—like the labyrinth the Minotaur hung out in? This one was typical, I guess, of outdoor ones on big estates: a confusing network of narrow paths between a lot of rows of spiny bushes, seven or eight feet tall, planted very close together. The turns made by the paths were all right angles, and many of them left you in dead ends. I imagine it was *possible* to get between the bushes, but you'd have to really force your way, and take a lot of scratches in the process. Having gotten in a maze, you almost always lose your way and get all turned around so that you can't tell where you started. What you have to do is keep on going though, using trial and error, and with a little patience you can reach the center—probably. I'd conquered this one, in the daylight, by myself, and so I knew that the center goal was like a little room, a nice square space, that had a little marble bench in it.

Now we walked around the thing until we reached the gap that was its entrance.

"Hey—race you to the middle!" Malcolm said. With which he dropped my hand, stepped through the gap, and took off to the right.

I was sure that that was wrong. I'd solved the thing two days before, and I remembered that you had to start out left. And so I did so, with a wicked laugh, flying down the narrow path between the bushes.

But soon enough I had to make another choice, and then another, and a third. Should I take that right, or keep on going? I could not remember, but I had to choose, and choose, and choose again. I found myself dead-ended, and retreated. Now where was I? Had I come from there—or *there*? That had to be the way, I thought, and went that way, to find that I was blocked again. It seemed that every path I took went nowhere.

I stopped and turned around again, and heard another set of footsteps coming quickly down a path exactly parallel to mine.

"Malcolm?" I said, not too loud. I didn't see how it could possibly be him, not there, not on that side of me. "There" was closer to the center, wasn't it? And certainly he hadn't *passed* me, had he? Or had I turned this way and that so many times I didn't know which way was "center" anymore?

"Malcolm?" I said—slightly louder this time.

The footsteps stopped. I heard some heavy breathing. Then there was a sound—and not a friendly one—a sort of snarl (or, possibly, a chuckle?), before the footsteps started once again. But now it seemed as if the person—Malcolm?—might have started panicking, or going slightly crazy. It sounded pretty much as if he now was bouncing off the bushy walls, or tearing at them in a frenzy. I heard a lot of crackling, some further gutturals, and scrambling.

Could some big animal have trapped itself in there? I wondered. But the running sounds had seemed the kind *two* feet would make, not four.

If any psychopathic killers had escaped from any nearby jails, I hadn't heard about it—but that was just because at Mycroft House we didn't listen to police short wave, the way my father always did; he'd know. Wouldn't it be just my luck, I thought, to lose the life I hadn't even found yet—and all because I'd left my home to look for it?

But now, I realized, the running, crashing sounds had stopped.

I took off the sandals I'd had on and started creeping down the path I had to take, trying not to make a sound. Every time I saw a "doorway" to another path, or reached a turn, I'd stop and stand there listening with all my might, hoping that my heartbeat wasn't audible to anyone but me. Whoever I had heard was *somewhere,* after all, either tiptoeing along, like me, or standing stock-still, waiting. So, every time I went around a turn, or stepped onto another path, I had to be afraid I'd find myself confronting it (or, more than likely, *him,* or *them*).

I'd just made still another stop when, from behind and to the right of me, there came a cry. It was the voice I'd feared I'd never hear again.

"Fleesh!" it called. "Fuh-leash-ee-yuh!" Yes, it was *Malcolm!*

"What!" I screamed—yes, *screamed*. "Oh, Mal, I'm over here! I'm lost!"

"I've made it to the *center,*" he called back. "It's neat. Come on. All you have to do is home in on my voice, okay? Let's see—what can I say? Or, how about I *sing* something? I know, I'll sing that song we used to sing at camp—'By the Silvery Moon.' Or wait, I know a better one. I'll sing 'A-Maze-ing Grace,' how would that be?" I bet my eyes bugged out, as in amazement, and I heard him laugh.

But before he started singing, I had started moving; oh, yes, yes, indeed I had. I made a few wrong turns, the way you always do (even with a voice to follow), but as he sang, I kept on getting closer, talking all the time. Like so:

"Here I come. I hear you loud and clear. Oops-oops, I made a bad choice that time. But now I'm going back, and *now* I'm on the right path, have to be. . . ." Just babbling away.

I suppose between the two of us we would have drowned out any sounds that anybody/anything was making, but to me the only thing that mattered was I kept on hearing him (he didn't have too bad a singing voice), and he, presumably, was hearing me. As long as I was talking, he would know my throat had not been cut and, more important, so would I.

I made one final turn and there he was, standing on that little marble bench, one hand laid on his heart, and singing like an angel—my deliverer! I don't think I've ever been so glad to see another human being.

And so I said, "Oh, Mal," and ran toward him, bawling.

Of course, I wouldn't know if he had ever played a scene like this before. I doubt it. But, either way, I will say this for Malcolm Warren: No one could possibly improve on how he handled both the situation and . . . well, *me*.

The first thing that he did was hop down off the bench and open up his arms, so I could run straight into them.

And once I had, he wrapped them tight around me and began to kiss my eyes, my lips, my nose, my cheeks, my chin—while telling me that everything was fine, and I was safe, and he'd take care of me.

I was amazed how quickly I stopped crying. Once in his arms, I took about a half a dozen gulps, and then my blubbering, the worst of it, was over. And almost before I knew it, we were sitting on the bench and I was kissing Malcolm back as . . . *ardently* (I guess) as he was kissing me.

It was fantastic. In less time than it takes to say "Jane Austen," the scariest place in the world was transformed into the most wonderful place in the world—this lovely, moon-bathed, *private* little room. The person I had heard (I told myself)—it simply must have been dear Malcolm, hastening to make it to the center of the maze, and to his rendezvous with *me*!

Now, it seemed to me, the maze *protected* us, from prying eyes and ears. No one would stumble on us there, returning from the movies or their parents' home. If we cared to, we could strip off all our clothes and chase each other round and round and on and off the marble bench (seeing how the moonlight painted both our slender bodies silver), till at last we fell, together, panting, on the greensward.

That wasn't what we *did,* of course, but still we did have fun. I must admit I learned some things—about myself, and boys, and *life* (I guess) in general. My mother would have been appalled by me, but not (I have to think) surprised, or in too towering a rage. Malcolm was terrific, never scary, and he *did* make great transitions. Long before we left that bench, I thought I was in love.

Of course I didn't say so, though; I'm a reader, so I know some things about the modern male. Such as: He's wary of commitments. And anyway, the thing I wanted wasn't something monumental, for all time. I wanted an *affair*.

Yes, what I wanted was a simple *love* affair. Unforgettable, perhaps unlawful, but basically unlasting, too. I was only (almost) seventeen, and not about to settle down, myself. I was a *writer,* loading up my pen with . . . yes, the blue ink of *experience*. Malcolm was—would be—"the first love" of my life. Perhaps, oh, years and years and *years* from now, we'd meet again—on Corfu, say, or possibly St. Kitts—and fall in love again, "forever." I wouldn't rule that out, but neither would I count on it.

For now, the only thing that mattered was the present.

What did that parrot (mynah bird?) say in that novel (story?) by either Alec or Evelyn Waugh (I'm pretty sure it was)? "Here and now, boys. Here and now." That was it, exactly: "Here and now."

Eight

I know my consciousness kicked out almost the moment that my right ear hit the Hollofil, a little after midnight. That was SOP, for me. I'm a stranger to insomnia, no matter what. Even on the first night of (smack lips) my "life."

But then, a shocker: I came wide awake at six A.M. And it was Saturday. I had the feeling I had slept my fill; I was eager to be "up and at 'em" (in my father's loathsome words—I leave the hateful pleasure in his voice to your imagining). What was going on?

At first I feared I might be coming down with something, *teen senility,* perhaps. My grampa says that he "don't need to sleep the way I useta." But then I got the idea it was something else. My love affair with Malcolm (smile) was changing me already, I believed. Now more complete, fulfilled, I didn't have to laze around in bed, avoiding life, long after I had logged what sleep my body needed to recharge its cells. Like Thomas Alva Edison's, my organism had become efficient. Now, I thought, I'd be Felicia-to-the-max, a human dynamo. A girl who sleeps hard, loves hard, works hard, plays hard. (What sounds are those I hear? Someone defooding, possibly? Can't say I really blame you.)

In any case, I rose, slipped on my terry robe, and headed for the kitchen, manuscript in hand. Five minutes later, there was coffee in the other hand, and I was in the servants' dining room. I was pretty sure I'd have four hours to myself, to work on my novella.

The night before, I realized, meant more than that my world had changed, excitingly, dramatically. It also meant that the action in real life (Felicia's "getting together" with Malcolm Warren) had *gotten ahead of* the action in my book (the Fiona–Martin Silverado pairing). Up until now, the imaginary events had presaged or foretold the real ones in a very near uncanny way. But it was as if *real life* had suddenly put on a sprint, to get ahead of literature. This, I thought, was something I should remedy at once. The other way was better; I had more control. (I'd really started thinking that I did.) Not that I didn't love the turn my life had taken, understand. It was something I had planned to try to cause to happen, when I put Fiona in the book. But be that as it may, I thought, I now should write real fast and, *one,* get

Annabel to somehow lose whatever yen she might have had for Martin Silverado (create some other, greater, "interest" for the girl?), and *two,* get Fee fixed up with him. And then go on from there.

If I didn't get ahead again, my precious book would surely be in danger of becoming just a *chronicle* of life in Mycroft House, and cease to be a work of fiction. Shudder.

With all those things in mind, I jumped right into Chapter Seven, in which Annabel and Martin and Fiona talked about the things they'd seen and heard over in the east wing of the castle.

They all agreed on one thing, right away: There was an artist over there, a painter. That smell was unmistakable and, at one time or another, they had all enrolled in Art at school. But there were still some harder questions to address. Such as:

Was the painter *Marge,* or the "Robed Figure"?

Whose room did the RF leave, and whose did he or she then enter?

Who'd been making all those groan-type sounds?

Martin Silverado shouted down the other two and gave his answers/explanations/theories first. Fiona thought they were . . . amusing—and quite typical of him: original, impulsive, and mistaken.

As Martin Silverado saw it, Marge, their hostess, was the painter, "hadda be." He said that "fit" with all the rest of her—the kind of person who would own a castle, write exotic cookbooks, and provide a sanctuary for a bunch of kids. She was the "off-the-wall eccentric artist type," he said; he'd known that from the moment he first heard of her. The Robed Figure that they'd seen had left the room that served as Marge's studio *and* bedroom. What they had overheard, he said, was "sociosexual interaction," by the two of them. Then, he said, they'd watched as the Robed Figure returned to her own room. Fiona noticed that he stressed the pronoun only very slightly; Martin Silverado was a worldly, open-minded boy.

But she, Fiona, while conceding that what he said was possible, said *she* didn't think that he was right. *She* thought the RF was a man, and Marge's lover, *and* the painter. She hypothesized that he was painting Marge—yes, in the nude, of course—but that his, well, artistic side kept fighting losing battles with his (shall we say?) *romantic* side. So, one thing kept on leading to some others (groans accompanying), after which Marge always fell asleep, and he went back to his own room, not being into painting naked corpses.

Annabel D. Day thought both of them were largely wrong—although Fiona had been right in two respects. The RF *was* the painter, and a male. But he was younger, maybe twenty-two or -three, and Marge's *son*. Like artists everywhere and since the start of time, he *suffered,* mightily. He'd contracted a disease, some parasite or other, in the jungles of Guyana, where he'd gone to paint a waterfall or something. They'd heard him groaning as he worked, said Annabel; his groans were part and parcel of the process of his giving birth to art—and also might have had to do with his intestinal disturbances. They had watched (or heard) him leave his studio, walk down the hall, and enter his own bedroom. Marge's room, she told them sagely, wasn't even on that *floor*.

Martin Silverado laughed and said he thought her explanation was "whacked out." He suggested that she ought to try her hand at writing teen romances—what an insult. His ideas, he said, had been the only "realistic" ones, although Fiona's, he admitted, had a certain "tang" to them.

Chapter Seven ended with Fiona and himself departing A.D.'s room and heading down the hall toward hers and his. They planned to get a little sleep before they had to rouse themselves again and head for school. As they said good night, outside her door, Martin told her he was sorry that he'd been so "forward" with her. He said he'd never felt that way before, been so "brought on" just looking at a girl. He promised that he'd try to be a "gentleman" henceforth.

Fee pulled the reed out from between her frosted lips and tapped him on the nose with it. "God rest you, merry gentleman," she purred. "Let nothing you dismay." And winked, and closed the door. She couldn't keep herself from toying with the guy.

Which brought me to the start of Chapter Eight. *It* began as follows:

8

Annabel D. Day was feeling pretty miffed when she turned out the light that night. She thought that her ideas—her explanation of the things they'd seen and heard—had been every bit as good as Martin's, or her friend Fiona's. The more she thought about it, in fact, the more she was convinced she *could* be right.

She was sure she knew as well as either of the others—maybe even *better*—how a groan of pleasure differed from a groan of pain. The first parts of both kinds of groans were very similar; it was at the *end* that they changed. The groans she'd heard that night had ended badly, she was sure.

And something else: The way the RF looked when going through that door—while entering the second room—gave credence to her theory, too. He'd done that in a way a *young man* would; there was no mistaking it. All she'd had to do was *hear* the forceful way he turned the knob, and *see* him put his vital shoulder to the door, and *feel* the little thrill his masculine determination brought to every nerve end in her body. She'd watched enough young men come into rooms through doors; she was sure she knew whereof she spoke.

During all of the next morning, as she went from class to class at school, and sat *in* class and practiced drawing elephants' behinds and different ways of signing her three names (Annabel D. Day, A. Donna Day, and A. D-with-just-a-squiggle), she thought about the argument they'd had. And how she'd like to prove that she was right, while proving Martin Silverado wrong-wrong-WRONG. By midday, she'd arrived at a decision. She was going to head back to the castle during lunch and see what she could see.

She did, and yes, the first thing that she saw was no Marge Costner's big old Cadillac. Not sitting right outside, not parked in the garage. Mrs. C., it seemed, had gone out shopping, or whatever. Excellent. And chances were, she'd taken that amazing Grace along with her, another good development. When it came to sneaking up and down a castle's halls, two feet, in Annabel's belief, were much better for the job than six.

So, first she used her heavy iron key and opened up the massive, studded, main front door. Double-checking, she approached the kitchen calling "Grace" and "Marge"; neither one replied. Thus satisfied, she set out on the route they'd trod the night before. She reached and passed through the Great Hall, and danced straight up the stairs as silently as mischief does in maidens' eyes. In daytime, even though the light was dim, she could see where she was going; at the far end of the corridor there was a narrow window of the kind, she thought, that bowmen used to fire arrows from (and also into, probably). The doors to all the rooms were closed, as usual, and nobody was groaning, anywhere.

Moving as quietly as possible in her cross-trainers, Annabel went down the hall, listening at every door. She heard nothing, anywhere. She came back up the hall again. She'd decided she would take a look inside the room that she was certain was "his" studio.

She held her breath as she reached out to grasp the doorknob. She touched it, clutched it, turned it, pushed. The door moved inward, and she followed it into the room. She smiled. It was a studio, all right. There was no bed in it, no cot, no chaise, no ottoman, no beanbag chair. There *was* a comfy-looking couch, but heck, so what? On an easel was the work-in-progress; Annabel suppressed a groan. It was no nude, not in any school of painting she had ever heard of, anyway. It looked more like a big balloon made out of bubble gum (perhaps), rising from behind a mound of (maybe) plastic peanuts.

"Well?" a voice said suddenly, and right in her left ear. And just as it said that, a pair of hands gripped both her arms above the elbows.

She couldn't turn her body, just her head. His face was right by her left shoulder, and she almost groaned again, the other kind. It was a gaunt, fine-featured face, its upper lip and cheeks and chin encrusted by a dark brown stubble, but its eyes were as soft and liquid as a Holstein's, or a thoughtful child's. He looked to be . . . oh, twenty-two or -three.

"Well—what?" she managed to get out.

"Well, how'd you like it?" he inquired. And stepping slightly to his left and forward, he both cocked his head a little to one side and changed his hold on her. Now the two of them were side by side; he had his right arm wrapped around her shoulder, pressing her against his side. You *could* say "hugging her," in fact.

"Very much," said Annabel D. Day, and she was telling him the truth.

"You're one of them from the west wing, I guess," he said.

"Yes," she said. "I'm Annabel."

"And I," he said, "am Dermott Costner, Marge's stepson."

There, I thought, when I had finished writing that. My mission was accomplished. I hadn't gotten Fee and Martin Silverado into kissing, but that didn't matter. And I surely had provided Annabel another focus (outlet, or whatever) for her well-maintained romantic energies.

I stood up and went into the kitchen, looked at the big clock in there: ten after ten already—yikes! It was time, past time, for me to move along, get into costume for the scene I hoped to play in next. Hastily, I went back into the dining room, scooped up my writing stuff, and hustled up the stairs.

Nine

In my room, I took out my freshly laundered, sleeveless, cotton, floor-length nightie—the very nearly see-through one with teeny buttons partway down the front—and headed for the bathroom. There, I showered, washed and dried and brushed my hair, and scrubbed my teeth and tongue. After that, I put the nightgown over just a pair of white v-kini briefs (with just a little lace on them), and headed down again, for "breakfast."

There was no one in the kitchen, still, and so I took my

time. The idea was to be there, bare-armed and adorable, and just beginning breakfast when the others—well, one other—first came down. I thought the odds were pretty good that Mal would get there next. It was a little nervous-making, my first "morning after," so to speak. Not that it was after all that much, but in the ordinary way of things, you might not see a boy you'd done stuff with the night before for . . . days sometimes. And there's always such a thing as "second thoughts," you know.

I wandered in the pantry, thinking I might have some cereal, eventually, that morning. Kate had bought a lot of different brands, and the boxes were lined up on the top shelf. What would Proust select? I asked myself. Or Plath? How about the Frosted Flakes? I reached for them, one arm extended, rising on my toes. If, perchance, a morning breeze had swirled in through the pantry window, hitting me, it would have surely found the ample armhole of my nightie, and caressed my small (but nice), and bare, right breast.

That was the pose—position—I was in when Malcolm snuck into the pantry, barefoot, grabbed my slender bod, and nuzzled my left ear. Because I'd sort of been expecting him, I didn't give a yell, or kick straight backward with my heel. Instead, I made a little happy sound—more gurgly than groanish—as I turned around and kissed him, liking how his hands moved on my back and sides, et cetera. He was dressed in shirt and pants, and he had also brushed his teeth and maybe even shaved. For sure, his face was very nice and smooth.

And then we both heard someone run the water in the kitchen sink. We quickly stepped away from each other, and *I* said, probably a bit too loudly, "Well, I think *I* want some Flosted Frakes."

To which *he* answered, "Me, I'm strictly go for Cap'n Crunch."

After that exchange, we strolled into the kitchen, bearing cereal and looking casual. Probably as casual as someone standing in a flashlight beam in someone else's house, and holding someone else's jewelry.

"Hey, look who's here!" said Allison. "And where did you two go last night?" She looked me over, took me in—the nightie *and* the blush that I'd been hoping wasn't showing. "You look as if you got a moonburn, Fleesh. Did you go to Brian Vogel's party? When I got back, there wasn't anybody here for me to play with." And she pushed her lips out in a big, exaggerated pout.

"No," I said, recovering. "You won't believe what *we* did." My mind went racing through the possibilities. I *was* the practiced liar, after all; this wasn't any job for amateurs.

"We *walked* to Sheila Wickenden's," I said. "*Someone* said that Sheila'd said it was her birthday and her folks were giving her a party as a present, a live band and everything. *Someone* said we could get a ride from lots of people, coming home, and it was a great night for a walk, and he bet that *you* might even stop there, when you finished with your calls."

"And," said Al, "what really happened?"

"What really happened was that just as we were getting there," I said, "*someone* remembered that the date today—that's yesterday, of course—was the fourteenth, and not the twenty-first. And that the twenty-first had been the date that Sheila'd said."

"Of course," said Allie. "I knew that."

"So, after that," I said, "we had a nice walk back. Of course, it seemed a little longer, even, coming back from way up there near Sheila Wickenden's. *Someone* insisted that we stop for ice cream. And that it was his treat. And that that would make us even." I looked at Malcolm with an evil leer. "*Someone* doesn't know me very well."

Everybody laughed at that, and soon the three of us were sitting down and having cereal and milk and juice and coffee. Afterward, I went upstairs to dress, and when I'd done so, I walked straight to Allie's room, and knocked, and entered. Call me unsophisticated, wet behind the ears, a doofus, or a masochistic moron, but I had to tell her. I do the same thing with my mother, all the time—feed her a nicely decorated three-layer lie, then yank it back before it's half digested, and substitute a plain hard roll of truth.

"We didn't walk to Sheila Wickenden's last night," I said as I came in. Ms. *Break-it-to-her-gently,* right? "We took a walk around the grounds, and I got panicked in the maze, which meant I guess he had to kiss me. And so I kissed him back a time or two. But, Al, I'm really sorry, and I absolutely promise you—*can* promise you—that I will cut the whole thing off, right now, if you have any interest in him, whatsoever, still."

(You possibly are wondering: Would she do that? Would she have done that, if her friend had asked her to? I honestly don't know. I like to think I would've, even if that meant I'd never have a life, or be a woman of the world. But maybe that's completely immature of me; shouldn't Malcolm have a say in this, somewhere? But let me say again: I honestly don't know.)

Allison was sitting down when I came in, painting her toenails. The color that she'd chosen I would call a *fuchsia,* but it could have been magenta. Now she gawked at me.

"You *what*? He *what*? Till after midnight? Sheesh, Feleesh, you sure must give long kisses." Then she grinned and said, "Hell, no. He's absolutely yours, all yours. And it isn't *just* that I don't want your rejects." She laughed. "The thing is that I didn't bring him here for that. I told you, Malcolm's more like . . . I don't know, a *cousin*. The kind of boy you think is pretty cute, and maybe kid around with, but who isn't someone you're all *juiced* about." She bent and picked up one of the white sandals she was going to wear.

"You say you *panicked,* Fleesh?" she said. She made that little tsk-tsk sound. "I'm ashamed of you. How *unoriginal,* and you a *writer,* too. I mean, talk about a Stone Age strategy. . . ." She laughed some more and shook her head.

I could feel myself begin to blush again, although I had no reason to—or not that reason, anyway.

"No," I said, "I really, truly did—get panicky, I mean. I was in the maze, and it was dark, and I was sure I heard somebody there. Somebody *else,* who wasn't Malcolm. And then when I couldn't find the path I wanted to be on . . . The feeling just built up and up. It was like when you imagine some guy's following you on a dark street, but you don't exactly *see* him when you turn around. But you keep going faster and faster, anyway. *You* know."

Allison was nice about it, once she saw that I was serious. She did try to extract, worm out, a few more details—get a little play-by-play description of the action in the maze, post-panic. But I wasn't too cooperative. I made it clear, however, that we hadn't *said* a lot of stuff, worked out the—what? parameters?—of our relationship.

"Chances are it's just a *fling,*" I said, with a most un-Fleeshly, off-hand, wave. "But *fun.*"

"A fling," repeated Allie. She had a pretty good idea of how much flinging I had done, historically, but still she didn't mock me. "And you're right. A fling can be more fun than anything. Just promise me you'll let me know"—she

had to grin again—"if someone ends up off her feet."

I smiled and nodded, waved again, and exited the room. I couldn't have been happier, and I was on a roll, I thought. And so I went to see if I could find Milady Kate.

I could and did. I found her out in what she called the "cutting garden." That's the garden where the lady of the manor goes to get the flowers she will later have in vases, here and there around the house. You don't cut flowers from the *other* gardens; they are there for looks, to look a certain way. To cut from them would ruin the effect. I'm sure you understand.

"Hi," she said, when I hove into view. "Good *morning*. Aren't these tulips lovely?"

They were, indeed. Big red and yellow ones, they were. So perfect they looked artificial—hold it, let me take that back!

I eased into my chosen subject slowly. At first I asked about the different flowers. What was that kind called? And how long did they bloom?

And then, "Did David plant all this? Does he do gardens, too?"

It seemed to me she almost burst out laughing.

"Oh, no," she said. "He isn't into flowers, much. I don't think they go with his self-image."

"I ran into him again, two days ago, I guess it was," I said. "When I was coming back from school. It looked like he was going on a bike ride."

"Yes," she said. "It seems that he's been getting into biking. I'm afraid he has a thing for speed."

"He must be quite an athlete," I said. "He's probably more interested in sports than digging ditches or making fieldstone terraces. He asked me to play tennis with him, actually—but I told him that I don't know how. He said he'd teach me if I wanted. I guess you let him use the court, and all. . . ."

Chances are Kate knew that I was being delicate. And that I'd really asked a question: "Do you let this loafer use your tennis court?"

"Yes," she said. She said it slowly: Yeh-ess, as if her mind were elsewhere. "I do." Then her head came up, and she began to speak more quickly.

"As a matter of fact," she said, "I'd been planning to talk to you and Allison and Malcolm. About . . . oh, David's *situation.* About *David.* Maybe we could get together after dinner. D'you think that that'd be all right?"

"Sure," I said. "I guess we could. We were maybe going out tonight, to Murray Lathrop's party, but, just speaking for myself . . ." I know that I was sounding like a little wuss, but we *were* moochers, after all.

"No, listen, *go,*" said Kate. She was what my mother *might* have called permissive, but instead had simplified to "crazy." "There really isn't any tearing hurry." She paused. "But how would . . . oh, tomorrow morning be? Or let's say *noon,* instead. You'd all be up and everything by noon on Sunday, wouldn't you? Or wouldn't you?"

"Oh, absolutely," I replied. She was being so darn nice, I almost couldn't stand it. "And I could talk to Al and Mal right now, and make sure that that's okay with them. All right?"

"Fine," she said. I had the feeling she was pleased—almost relieved—this subject had come up. "I'll be here or

in the pantry, getting them"—she gestured toward the pile of flowers in her basket—"into water."

Allison and Malcolm both said Sunday noon was fine with them. Of the two, Malcolm seemed more puzzled, or surprised, that there was any need to talk about some kid he hadn't even seen, who worked there on the grounds. But, sweetie that he is, he just said, "Fine." So I, the faithful little messenger, reported three "okays" to Kate.

I could start another sentence here by saying "Little did I know . . . ," but that would be too corny and clichéd a thing for someone like myself to say. Writers like Joyce Carol Oates and I do not use "Little did I know . . . ," and for good reason. I'm sure you will agree.

Ten

We did go to Murray Lathrop's party, that same night, all three of us, together—not, strictly speaking, a ménage à trois, but more than merely housemates. Allie drove us, though the Lathrops' house was not that far. She said she had a little headache and would want to have the car, in case she started feeling worse.

Probably the party wasn't all that bad. If I had gone to it two weeks before, the chances are I would have told my mom, next day, that it was "okay"—not great, not terrible.

By that I would have meant I ate and drank my fill of mostly orange-colored junk, heard some music that I liked as well as some I couldn't stand, watched two guys behave like total idiots (while thinking they were oh-so-cool and "having fun"), and faced the fact, again, that Justin Sargent wasn't ever going to be my Jordan Paradise.

But because it wasn't two weeks earlier, I thought the party was almost a total groan. I didn't want to eat Cheese Doodles, or scream "Marsh!" at Marcia Levin just because she'd just screamed "Fleesh!" at me. And most of all I didn't want to spend a second of the night with Justin Sargent, who, about half an hour after we arrived, strolled over to my side and began to tell me all about the piece that he was working on for Writing Workshop. That, of course, sent Malcolm off to look for . . . something. Food, or drink, or Tylenol, another woman—*I* don't know.

It really was ridiculous. Here was Justin, shouting to make himself heard over the music, reciting all this crap about how Glen, his latest antihero, planned to "off" Lieutenant Simpson on their next reconnaissance patrol . . . as if I didn't know what he was really trying to do.

He was trying to hit me with his plotting skills (which Ms. Kevorkian had once, but only once, commended to the class), until I got all starry-eyed and rubber-legged (and weak of will, presumably), at which point he would lead me out onto the terrace, there to do his blundering and tense reconnaissance inside my silky-soft chemise—and maybe even send his awkward hand onto the no boy's (by the name of Justin) land beneath my chambray skirt.

What he didn't know—poor simp—was that he didn't have a chance, that night, of touching any part of me: no wow-ful corner of my mind, no square inch of my body. All

I could think about was Malcolm—who he was and where he was and how he was, and when he would be ready to get out of there and join me in a party of our own devising. It wasn't that I planned to drag him into *bed* (or the equivalent)—I was far from sure I wanted to, and we had yet to even *mention* birth control—it was more that this relationship was so completely new to me, so *tasty,* that I couldn't wait to take some further nibbles at it.

I got a lucky break when Allie came and dragged me off, away from Justin. She said her headache had got worse, and she was leaving; did I want to go? Before I asked the question I was framing in my head, she said that Malcolm said he wanted to *walk* home, and wondered if I wouldn't keep him company.

"He said he hoped you hadn't been recruited by 'the Sargent,' " Allie told me, leering as she did. And then she turned and took her headache out of there.

I needed quite a while to find where Malcolm'd disappeared to. I didn't want to ask a lot of people if they'd seen him anywhere. There's nothing more pathetic than a girl who's looking for a "missing" boyfriend at a party. Most of the time, though people won't admit they know his whereabouts, they do—and also who he's with, and even why. I was pretty sure that Malcolm wasn't hiding, or with someone else. And I also didn't want to advertise the fact that he and I were now an item. I am not a candy store, and so I've never liked a lot of noses pressed against my windows. And anyway, a fling, I thought I understood, was like a fireworks display. Although it took your breath away, it wasn't *meant* to last and last, while everybody talked about it, took it all apart, and tried to figure out what made it tick. A fling might burn out fast, but it would leave behind, on someone such as me (I thought), an aura of *experience,* a glow that made a statement to the world: "She's been around; she

knows."

Eventually, I reached the Lathrop kitchen, where I found "my man" discussing either . . . metaphysics or the Boston Red Sox (was it?) with four other boys. I didn't interrupt, or even say a word, in fact. I just passed calmly through the room and went on out into the night, by way of the back door. There, I waited, leaning up against a post that held up one end of the Lathrops' clothesline. In my head, I was reciting "Jabberwocky," that peculiar poem by Lewis Carroll. And before I'd finished the fifth verse ("One, two! One, two! And through and through/ The vorpal blade went snicker-snack/ He left it dead, and with its head/ He went galumphing back"), Malcolm came galumphing out of the kitchen door himself, looking very much as if he hoped to see me.

In just about the time it takes to do full justice to the term "a warm embrace," the two of us, with arms locked tight around each other's waist, had started on our way to Mycroft House.

And a most delightful walk it was. From time to time, we stopped and kissed along the way, and I felt quite depraved, being so . . . *outrageous* on a sidewalk by a public thoroughfare, where *anyone* might come along and see us. I suppose I also felt a little disappointed that nobody did. When, at last, we'd wandered up the driveway and the house came into view, we saw that Allie's car was parked where it belonged, and that her bedroom light was off. Kate's car was also in, and her wing, too, was dark. We tiptoed through the big front door—in hopes that Roger would be upstairs on Kate's bed and fast asleep—and finally (safely) reached the big, down-pillowed sofa in the living room.

Our couch time also was a real delight. We were less *potatoes* than *zucchini, melons,* and *tomatoes*—things you'd find on *vines*. And as we twined around, and sent out runners over each other, we exchanged a lovely range of compliments, and *adorations,* even. Malcolm, it turned out, had had (for months and months) a secret yen for this Felicia Gordon, writer. But (he said) he'd feared that a girl of my attainments (in addition to my "sensual" good looks) would never "get it on" with some "dumb sod" like him. Answering, I put my finger on his lips and whispered he was "my Apollo," bringer of the sunlight to my life, and that he shouldn't call himself a "sod." (Although, absurdly maybe, I kept thinking "terra firma" as we ground ourselves against each other.)

Oh, yes, it was a lovely evening—though I suspect it sounds like total slop to anyone who wasn't there. Before we headed up to our own rooms, we had to (I'll now use a favorite word of Justin's) *redeploy* our clothing some, but that seemed simply suitable, and not at all embarrassing, or odd. Although I wasn't sure I'd ever choose to be Apollo's lover/mistress/bride, I definitely was loving all the things I got to do and feel while I was making up my mind.

At three minutes before noon on Sunday morning, Allison, Malcolm, and I walked out of Allie's room and headed for the terrace. I'm not sure about the others, but I know I felt uneasy and a little on my guard. It was I who'd had the bright idea that we should all go down together.

It might be that my nervousness was rooted in . . . say, *history*. At home, at school, and even on the job I'd had (working as a grocery checker at the Northfield Mall), whenever someone in power called a special meeting, it was very apt to mean there was a *problem,* and that *change* was on the way. I didn't think I'd welcome any changes in the setup or routine at Mycroft House. So far, events that had transpired there had merely equaled or surpassed my wildest dreams.

It was warm that Sunday, and everybody had on shorts. Kate carried out big pitchers of iced coffee and iced tea, and put them on the glass-topped table. Then she went back for glasses, sugar, cream, and napkins, insisting that she didn't need our help. After that, she made another trip, for spoons, but barely had sat down again before she said, "Oh, *lemon,*" and went to fetch some slices, on a plate. I was pretty sure that that took care of everything, but Kate then said she'd made some sandwiches, egg salad and roast beef, which she could get if anyone was hungry *now.* We all said no, we'd wait: I'm sure my smile looked frozen on my face. By then, I would have gladly tied her to her chair.

"Well, then," said Kate. And she began to talk, at last, blurting out the first few things she had to say.

"I suppose I ought to start by telling you I've lied to you." She did that in one breath. "Or *sort of* lied by leaving out some stuff, concerning David. I'm really sorry, but I thought I had to." And she paused, and talked a little slower after that.

"First of all," she said, "he isn't just a kid who works here, on the grounds; David is my brother. And second, I should tell you that I didn't ask you here because—or *just* because—I wanted company myself. Or on account of I'm the world's most generous, agreeable woman. Or even for the simple reason that I'd heard the three of you are much the nicest people in your age group in the entire country." She gave a little laugh that sounded forced, to me. "Though, honestly, *I* am—and so are you, *of course.*

“No,” and here she stretched her long tan legs way out and pointed her bare toes. She had on another pair of tailored linen shorts. “I asked you here because I hoped that you might help him, help my brother, David. He could use some friends right now, I think; he needs to be around good people. People like yourselves. I know you won’t be living here that long, but any time is long enough to make a start, to get a process going.”

When I heard that, I kept on staring fixedly at Kate, determined that I wouldn’t do the one thing I felt most like doing, which was checking out how Al and Mal were taking this—this little bombshell, as I thought of it. My trouble was, I *liked* Kate Mycroft, so I didn’t want to make her feel she wasn’t one of “us.” I’m sure that we make teachers feel that way a lot, when “we” look back and forth at one another, in that certain way; I know that parents find it irritating lots of times. As if they’re up against a set of people they can never be a member of.

But, at the same time, I did experience a certain letdown. It seemed that Kate had done a number on me, on the three of us. She’d done a thing that adults do to kids a lot: They keep, oh, certain things from kids because they aren’t sure (the grown-ups aren’t) that the kids can “handle” them (the things). We kids are sort of made to pass a test that takes a certain length of time, a test that we don’t even know we’re taking. In the case of this particular space of time, a friendship was established. And now it seemed to me that Kate was asking us to put the feelings that we had for her to work for David. Someone who we didn’t feel the same about at all. Was that *fair*? I asked myself. Was it right for her to do that to us? And you know another thing that stunk? I didn’t know the answers to those questions.

Meanwhile, Kate had kept on talking. "Here's the story," she had said.

It seems there'd been an "accident," where they had lived before, "back home" (in Indiana, or wherever it was), an auto accident involving David. He'd been hurt quite badly in it, she explained, "a head injury," among other things; he'd had a slow and painful convalescence. His memory had been affected; he'd forgotten lots of things he'd learned before, both in and out of school. He had, she said, no recollection whatsoever of that day, or of the accident itself. According to the doctors whom they'd seen, it was more than likely that he never would remember *it* (though other things would constantly come back to him). And the doctors all agreed that that was just as well.

"I'm not trying to be mysterious," said Kate. "But I don't think there's any point in going into all the gory details. David knows he was in a wreck and that he almost died. He doesn't seem to want to—need to—know much more than that. He never talks about what happened, and I'd hope you wouldn't bring it up with him—that's *if* you go along with what I'm getting ready to suggest to you. . . ."

Well, at that point my resolve broke down. I had to look at Allie. She had seen this David wearing nothing but a pair of skimpy swimming trunks. Surely she had noticed how his wrists were scarred. Hadn't she deduced (the same as me) that he had tried to kill himself? Was I wrong to be upset that Kate was lying to the three of us (again)?

And I was sure that she was lying; I could tell. It wasn't just the scars. There was something in her manner, something . . . *I* don't know, *evasive* in the way she looked—and she didn't look directly in our eyes. I'd heard that sometimes people were *ashamed* if someone in their family attempted suicide; I think my mother told me that.

Allie didn't look at me, however. She just kept on staring hard at Kate, taking all this in. Malcolm, on the other hand, was shifting in his seat, and when I'd turned to look at him, he'd started blinking; *he* seemed pretty ill at ease. He caught my eye and made a little face, one I took to mean "What *is* all this?"

Kate had gone on talking, saying how she hoped that maybe David could become a member of our little social group—have dinner with the rest of us, hang out with Al and Mal and me those times we weren't studying, or going out to be with other friends. She said he wasn't "ready" yet for school, or crowds of kids at parties, or a job, outside. He wouldn't—not in any way—be our "responsibility," she said.

"Is he—well—living in the house right now?" asked Mal. I'd been wondering the same, remembering the voices he and Al had heard.

"Oh, he has a room just down the hall from mine," said Kate. "He's got his own TV in there, a little fridge, a microwave—a lot of stuff like that. And sometimes he camps out. As a rule, I have my breakfast and my lunch with him, the days that you're at school. He wasn't all that thrilled about your coming here, to tell you the truth, but I persuaded him to give it a fair trial. I promised him he wouldn't have to have a thing to do with you unless he wanted to."

"And now he says he does?" I asked.

"Well, sort of," Kate replied. "I didn't want to say too much to him until I'd talked to you—*with* you. But he's expressed some very positive opinions on the three of you. Especially about *you,*" she said to me. "He thinks you're a really friendly person."

"*Everyone* likes Fleesh," said Allie, right away, with this repulsive little smirk smeared on her face. “That’s such a typical reaction.” I looked daggers back at her, which made her switch to an enormous grin, and reach way out to pat me on the knee. Of course, I had to grin myself, although I felt as if I might be drowning in a sea of bullshit.

“I haven’t even *met* him,” Malcolm said, “so I don’t know how he’d feel anything about me, one way or the other. But it’s his house, I guess you could say, so he ought to be able to do whatever he wants here—that’s what *I* think, anyway. I mean, most of the time we’re here, we’re either sleeping or studying, I guess.” And he sort of shrugged, and smiled at Kate as he was doing so.

This, I thought, was Malcolm being Malcolm, the boy his parents brought him up to be; the “right thing” was important to the Warrens, much more so than one’s own feelings. I thought he probably wasn’t all that thrilled by the prospect of having a strange boy become a part of our routines. After all, the reports he’d heard concerning David, from both Allie and myself, had hardly been what I’d call glowing. But he was being a *good sport*—in spite of how that might affect our cozy little “thing.”

Allie rose to pour herself some iced coffee.

“We aren’t going to be here all that long,” she said while adding cream. “But if you think we possibly could *help* him . . .” She shrugged, as if she had some doubts about that possibility, but still would *try*.

I was a bit surprised by this reaction. But then, I thought about—remembered—what I’d felt before: that she and Kate were fellow tribesmen (Malcolm, too), and that Kate was, after all, her *parents*’ friend, as well as hers, and she was more or less responsible for Mal and me, and this was something all of us were being *asked* to do, like as a *favor.* (I also realized that Allie had her car, and could bug out of there, away from David, anytime she wanted to, and fast.)

So that left me. How could *I* object? Plus, for all I knew, David might be lying underneath some nearby bush, taking all this in.

You can guess the rest. Before the sandwiches came out, we'd all agreed; there would now be five of us, instead of four. Kate suggested David join *her* cook-and-clean-up crew, hers and *Allie's* team. That handed me a chance to smirk at Al, even as I said that even though that gave *them* an extra pair of hands, it clearly was the way to go.

After, we met briefly, just the three of us, back in Allie's room again. I told them what my best guess was, concerning David, that he'd tried to slit his wrists—*had* slit his wrists—and was a mental case. I said I doubted that there'd ever been an auto wreck.

"What?" said Mal. "You told me he was strange, but you never said he'd tried to *kill* himself. How loony *is* this kid? You think he's safe to be around? No kidding."

Allie made a little "down, boy" gesture with her hand. "Easy does it, Malcolm," she advised. She put on a teachy-preachy tone. "Let's not forget whose theory you're about to swallow whole. Let me remind you that it could be someone's little *fantasy* that you've just heard. Felicia *likes* to make up stories, doesn't she? She could be full of it. She often is. He could have gotten those same scars a lot of ways." She paused for the effect. "Like going through a windshield, for example."

I shrugged and grinned. She could be right. A lot of things were *possible*. Including what I'd said.

"So, he doesn't say that he's Napoleon?" said Mal. "Or claim the FBI is programming his mind?"

"Nah," said Allie. "He's obnoxious. So're lots of people; think about our class at school. Probably, deep down, he's insecure and bashful, and he acts like that to cover up the way he really feels."

"Yeah, *right,*" I said. "He sure is *bashful.*" I was thinking of the fact that every time we'd seen the guy, he'd more or less been showing off the goodies.

But Allie only laughed and said it wouldn't kill us to do Kate a favor, after all.

There wasn't any way to disagree with that.

Eleven

Leaving Allie's room, I got this feeling that the characters and goings-on at Mycroft House were starting to bear at least a vague resemblance to those you'd find in daytime TV "dramas." All of us were *young,* or young enough, and one of us was surely *restless,* when the episodes began—impatient with her lack of life experience. And now the guy who'd only lurked around the edges of the action in the early scenes was about to come to center stage, somewhat unmasked.

Yes, David, we now knew, was not some local ne'er-do-well, who did a bad job working on the grounds; he was Kate's *brother.* But he was still "mysterious." Was he a nut case, or the convalescent victim of a major accident? Would his presence in the group pollute the easygoing atmosphere of Mycroft House? Stay tuned.

Hmm, I thought. David might be joining us at any time, perhaps as early as that very night. Interactions would ensue. Relationships, both good (?) and bad, would probably develop. So, didn't it *behoove* me (nice?) to grab my manuscript and get some fiction down on paper, first and fast? As you may recall, David's alter ego, the painter Dermott Costner, had recently come side to side with Annabel D. Day. But I had yet to tell my readers (Ms. Kevorkian, *perhaps* selected members of the class, and, with any luck, my literary executors) anything about the guy. Like why he groaned, and what odd wind had blown him to the castle. Clearly, time was (as they say) "a-wasting."

So, just minutes later, I was sitting at the tin-topped table by the pool in back of Mycroft House, shaded by the big umbrella that impaled said table through its very heart. Soon, I started scribbling some notes—my chapter outline. And, within another half an hour, I was writing. Chapter Nine, it was, as follows:

9

''Although I've *taken* art, I'm no authority,'' said Annabel D. Day. ''Except I know why different paintings work for me, and how. I can tell you this right now, in total honesty: I'm enlightened and excited. Yes, I really am.''

She was looking at the painting, at this (almost surely) latex moon, rising over quite a heap of (could be) Styrofoam. For the moment, she was loath to meet his eyes.

"Thank you *very* much," said Dermott Costner. The two of them were seated now, in two director's chairs. The canvas seats and backs of both had once been brown, but now they were a speckled mass of many dried-out colors, from the many times the artist had, both accidentally and on purpose, gotten paint on them.

"It's taken me a while to be the painter that I am today, to make this kind of statement, knowing that it won't be . . . *misunderstood.*" As he spoke, he pointed at the painting with two fingers, which he then moved quickly up and down, as if to play a trill upon the empty air. "Believe me, that feels good."

Annabel first nodded, understandingly. "I'll *bet* it does," she said. She paused. "So, if you can forgive my curiosity . . . I'd really like to know. I've heard you groaning in the night. In addition to the pleasure, there's some pain you're feeling, too?" Just wait, she thought, till Fee and Martin heard how very near right-on she'd been!

She watched him smile a smile like none she'd ever seen before, in terms of bravery and beauty. One saw no smiles like that at Southport High, not even on the faces of the student council, or the fencing team, or of the members of the drama club.

"Oh, sure," he said. "There's part of me that's hurting, still and badly. I guess there always will be. When I work, my mood goes up and down the scale of feeling, from the peaks of ecstasy to chasms of despair. And back again. And so on."

Annabel let out a bit more line. "How long have you been painting, then?" she asked.

"Two years and—let's see—fourteen weeks," he said. "I'd never touched a brush till I went in the . . . hospital."

Her eyebrows bungeed up her forehead in delight. "The hospital?" she said. "Don't tell me you were stricken with an illness carried up from . . . *South America,* perhaps?"

Now it was Dermott's turn to look surprised.

"I guess you *could* say that," he said. "It was rehab I was in. You're looking at a junkie, Annabel. I was addicted. To a sweet young girl named Adeline and then, by way of her, to crack cocaine." He looked down at the floor between his knees, and now his eyes, she saw, were hot springs, welling up with sadness.

"Do you want to talk about it?" she inquired softly.

"She was a golden girl," he started, head still down, "everybody's darling, queen of everything they ever made a crown for in our town. *I* was a nothing—quiet, nearly friendless all through school, a member of the stamp club. Chances are you know the type."

Annabel D. Day *did* know that type. Not personally, of course, but she still nodded.

"I was two years ahead of her, and out of school, working for an answering service, hoping to find something that I'd like to do as a career. 'Dr.

Jensen's office,' I would say. Or, 'Bullard, Dreyfus and Mahoney,' or 'Selby's Septic Service.' And then I'd write down whatever message the caller wanted to leave, things concerning medicine, or legal work, or sanitary systems. I learned a lot that way, but nothing seemed to *click*. Until the day that I met Adeline . . ." Dermott shook his head.

"It was raining; I had my umbrella, quite a good-sized black one. I was heading home from work, I guess. And she was standing in a doorway, waiting for the rain to stop. When I passed by, she started singing 'Gimme Shelter,' a cappella, no mean feat. You know the song? It's by the Rolling Stones. And so of course I offered to escort her home, or anywhere she wanted, under my umbrella. That was how it all began. All the time, I barely could believe that this was happening—that a girl as popular as Adeline would risk it all by being seen with me. And not just once, but many times thereafter. Although it wasn't long before I found out why."

"Why she more or less came on to you that day?" asked Annabel, more curious than ever. "Why she *chose* you, you could say?"

"Exactly." Dermott Costner nodded. "She *chose* me, as you put it, just because I was exactly who I was, a nobody, a nothing. I was *below* suspicion, not above it. No one would ever think that I was 'up to' *anything*. And Adeline—this paragon, this student council princess-president, this why-can't-you-be-like for kids for miles around—was way, way into drugs."

"Wow," said Annabel D. Day. "And you could be the

source of her supply? You could get the stuff from shady characters, and pass it on to her?"

Dermott Costner looked at her with burgeoning respect. "It isn't only *painting* you see clearly," he remarked. "That is *precisely* what she had in mind. You know . . ." His artist's eyes grew narrow as he stared at her. She felt that stare, as it took in the surface of her face, and of her upper body, and her torso, and her legs. And then went deeper, passing through her skin and body fat and muscle tissue, down until it reached the very structure of her bones.

"You know," he said again, "you look a lot like Adeline. You could be her younger sister, even." His eyes got softer, then more thoughtful, and he smiled. "Except—you *are* clean, aren't you?"

"Oh, I am, I am," said Annabel. "I used to do karate; no one tells me what to do, or calls me 'chicken.' I've taken puffs, and once I had a half a can of beer; I didn't like that, either. It isn't that I'm scared of drugs; it's more that I think doing them is stupid. I have a lot of other . . . interests." And she looked into his eyes, and smiled, herself.

"Including one extremely recent one," she said. "That's in this story you've been telling me. You started getting drugs for Adeline? And then you started taking them yourself?"

"Yes, typically and shamefully, I did," said Dermott Costner. "Instead of helping her, I joined her in this secret life of hers. No one suspected anything—except that Adeline was being *wonderful*, as usual, by being friendly to a friendless person. Indeed, the minister made mention of that fact, in just those words, while speaking at her funeral."

"Her *funeral*?" gasped Annabel D. Day. Her eyes resembled two white Frisbees, big and round with horror. "Adeline is *dead*? From an OD?" Although A.D. was shocked and horrified, she was also hostess to some other feelings, excited ones that landed in the middle of her chest, and there bounced up and down in wild abandon.

"No, hardly that," said Dermott. "Though she was plenty high when she cashed in. It happened in her car. Adeline was driving; she insisted. She wasn't going very fast; the skid marks on the road confirmed that. Possibly the steering was defective; possibly a tie rod broke. In any case, before I knew it, we were off the road, pinwheeling down into a gully, far below. Neither of us had seat belts on. When we hit bottom, I was all banged up, but Adeline was dead; her neck was broken. I never will forget that moment, in that night." And Dermott Costner groaned.

It was the twin to all those groaning sounds that Annabel had heard before (except she'd heard *them* from a distance). Or, if not the twin, at least a same-sex sibling. It made her have this thought: Although he didn't die that night, his life is still in danger. She wished they weren't seated in director's chairs; there was no way she could get her arms around him. And she didn't think "There, there" would do the trick.

He wasn't finished talking, though. He had to tell her the entire story. As it happened, he had done no drugs the day the tragedy occurred, and so, although concussed and with a broken clavicle, as well as cuts and bruises, he determined there was one last thing that he could do for Adeline. He would say that he'd been driving. No one would ever do a blood test on her then (he figured); she would never even be regarded as a "careless driver." Adeline, in death, would still (and always) be the nonpareil that she had been in life.

What Dermott didn't reckon on was the reaction in their town. Though there were never any charges brought against him by the cops, in everybody else's eyes he was no better than a murderer. He'd plucked the fairest flower from their midst, and there were those—her father and her brothers, two uncles and six cousins, a dozen members of the high-school faculty, and fourteen town and county politicians (as well as countless unrelated juveniles)—who said "some way, somehow" her death would be avenged.

So, Dermott then had done what almost anybody in that situation would have done: He took off, running. His initial hope was just to make it out of town, but once he had accomplished that, he had to settle on a destination. The one he chose, and mostly out of desperation, was quite a ways away. His father's second wife, named Marge, had always been real good to him (his were not *her* genes), and they had stayed in touch, even after Dermott's dad divorced her and began to date investment bankers.

Dermott knew that Marge had been remarried, to one Amos Costner, multimillionaire, who'd died and left her mistress of a castle in the town of Southport.

The kindly Marge not only took him in, giving him her name to hide behind, she also handed him the funds to put himself in treatment. The treatment worked; he had been clean for almost three years now and—as Annabel had seen—had made it as a painter.

"I don't know if they're still trying to find me," Dermott said to her. "I've cut my hair and grown this little stubble-beard, and I've also lost some weight and taken on—affected—certain mannerisms when I'm out in public. And, most of all, I'm now *successful*, something that they *never* thought I'd be. But even if they got their hands on me"—he sighed—"there's no new pain they could inflict on me that I would truly feel. I am numb, devoid of nerve ends. When Adeline ceased breathing, much of me expired, too." He lolled back in his chair and closed his eyes.

Annabel got up and walked around in back of him. She knew what she was going to have to do.

Perhaps he heard her footsteps. With his head still thrown way back, he opened up his eyes and found her standing over him, and looking down at him.

"I'm Annabel, not Adeline," she said. "*I* have a question for you. Do you *want* to be completely whole—alive again?"

"Yes," he said. "Oh, yes. I think I do."

So she bent down, and held his tired face in both

her hands, and started giving mouth-to-mouth resuscitation.

That was where my outline ended, with that big fat smooch. I knew I wouldn't have much trouble going on from there. Maybe, next, I'd write some nice Fiona–Martin Silverado action. It seemed as if my book was on the verge of getting pretty sexy, but that didn't bother me. Because I'd gotten more experience, myself, I was more confident that I could do a sex scene justice. And also, Ms. Kevorkian had told us to be "frank and truthful" when it came to our descriptions of relationships. ("Don't worry," she had told us. "I am *not* your Aunt Prunella.") I *did* feel a little strange about having Annabel, my Allison's equivalent, come on to Dermott in the way she did. But then I told myself I absolutely did not believe that everything I'd ever write would have its parallel in actual real life. And besides, hadn't Allie *said* she didn't care for David?

In any case, I started to reread the pages that I'd done, and found that I was feeling pretty pleased with Dermott Costner's "story." True, I'd borrowed just a little from the *David Mycroft* story, or at least the one that Kate had tried to sell us. But, by adding drugs and a girlfriend, and then killing off the girlfriend, I'd made it really different. It seemed to me I'd done some pretty fancy *plotting* there. Wouldn't Justin Sargent absolutely poop his pants (I thought), if Ms. Kevorkian began to compliment *another* person's storytelling skills?

My wallow in that pleasant fantasy did not last long, however. All of a sudden, came the sound of running footsteps, followed by a splash. I looked up. The surface of the pool now rocked and rolled. But when a head did not appear, I got a little anxious. Whoever it had been might possibly have hit his head—or hers.

I got up, walked over to the pool. On the way I thought: Suppose I need to rescue someone from the depths, would it be cool to drop my walking shorts before I dove or jumped? What underpants, I asked myself, had I put on that morning?

Luckily, I didn't have to come to a decision (it would have been a pretty hard one: Although my briefs were lace-trimmed cuties, they'd have been transparent, just about, when they got wet). When I got poolside and peered down, what did I see but David, sitting on the bottom, with a good grip on the drain, and looking up, and . . . *signing,* in a way. (*Rudely?* you inquire; well, my mom would say so.)

I knew he couldn't see me, so I turned and raced back to my seat. I'd barely reached it when his head resurfaced, with a whoop. I pretended that I'd only just looked up.

"Oh, hi," I said. "I *thought* I'd heard someone dive in. And then there wasn't anyone at all."

He pulled himself out of the pool and walked in my direction, tossing back his hair, and dripping. He had on either the same pair of trunks that Allie'd seen him in, or another pair, the next size smaller. I brought my eyes up to his face and kept them there.

"Boy!" he said. "I could have *drowned,* and you'd have kept on"—he looked down at my clipboard—"writing—what?—a *letter?*" He'd obviously assumed that I would run over to the pool and see his greeting, from the bottom. Tough buns, amigo. But he was not the first to underestimate Felicia.

"Not exactly," I replied. I didn't want to start explaining

what I do to him. I tried to think of something . . . (what had Kate said *he* had said about me?) *friendly?*

"You having dinner with the gang tonight?" was all I could come up with. I just assumed that he and Kate had talked.

"I might," he said. He turned away again and walked on over to the diving board. My eyes could finally leave his head, and did.

He hopped up on the board and walked out to the end of it, and started bouncing up and down.

"You want me to?" he said. He didn't turn his head to look at me, just kept on with his bouncing, going a little higher every time, and keeping his feet together, and pointing his toes on the way up.

"Well, sure," I said. "We all do. It'll mean another person helping out with dishes." And I laughed my friendly laugh.

"I want to learn to *cook,*" he said. Now he only spoke as he went up. "Instead of . . . just stick stuff . . . into the microwave. D'you know how . . . to make . . . a birthday cake? In case . . . I have . . . another birthday?"

"Sure, I guess," I said. "Although I may not be here when you do."

"You know," he said, "I may not, either."

And with that he gave a final bounce that sent him really soaring, seemingly straight up. When he'd gone as high as he was going to go, he brought his knees up to his chest, and wrapped his arms around them, and began to somersault. He spun so fast it was confusing; I couldn't really count the revolutions. But just before his falling, spinning body crashed down on the diving board, it snapped straight open and his pointing fingers broke the surface of the water, followed by the length of him, and finally by his pointed toes. He only missed the board by inches. I'd never seen a dive as good as that before.

I rose and picked my stuff up off the table, and headed for the house.

And as I did, I said "Nice dive" to him, instead of "Hey—you could have killed yourself."

Twelve

To say that David soon became a part of "us" would be not only true but, in a sense, an understatement. It wasn't only that he popped up everywhere, it was also what I guess you'd call his *style*.

He gave us our first taste of it that very night at dinner. In fact, he even joined "the gang" beforehand, in the kitchen.

It was Kate's and Allie's night as cooks, so they were being busy and responsible, while Malcolm and I lounged around pretending to give orders and find fault—acting like the lord and lady of the manor. I noticed Mal did better at all that than I did, no doubt because his parents always had provided him with live-in help, whereas *my* parents provided *themselves* with live-in help, by having me.

At the moment David made his entrance, the roast chicken was sitting on a platter (while its juices "set," I think Kate said). "I'll do the honors, Martha," Malcolm volunteered as he took out the carving knife and matching fork. He called both Kate and Allie "Martha" on the nights they cooked, in honor of some favorite *domestique* the Warrens once employed. Allie was pouring dressing on the salad she'd assembled in the king-sized wooden bowl, and Kate had put the roasting pan back on the stove, preparatory to adding flour to the fat she'd left in it, on the way to making gravy.

"So—whatcha doin'?" David asked his sister that as he came rushing in; he made a beeline to her side. The rest of us could easily have been invisible.

Kate had the heaping tablespoon of flour in her hand. "I'm going to sprinkle this in there, and then take that"—she nodded at a whisk—"and mix 'em up together. Then I'll put in *that*"—this time she pointed to a measuring cup of broth she'd made by boiling the chicken neck and gizzard and liver with an onion and a carrot and a stalk of celery—"and we'll get gravy."

"Ah!" said David, picking up the whisk. "Let *me* make that. That sounds like fun." He started stirring the flour and the melted chicken fat together, making this sort of yellowish-brown paste. "I *like* making *this,*" he said. "It's *fun.*" And he laughed a little more . . . triumphantly than necessary, I thought.

"Oh, put a sock in it," said Kate, more crossly than his

laughter warranted, perhaps; I figured she was nervous, this first night. I also snuck a look at Allie. She had made a face, and I wondered how many other people—other than the two of us—knew that the French word for the pasty stuff David was "making" was *roux,* spelled just the same as Allison's last name.

He surely wouldn't know, I told myself. He'd said he didn't know thing one, concerning cooking. But then I wondered: Would he? Surprises seemed to be a specialty of his.

In any event, we were soon sitting down to a first-class meal, including gravy, during which Mal, Allie, and I tried to do our best with David.

Malcolm was the least successful, I would say, right from the moment that he said, "You want to carve?" to David, offering the special knife and fork.

"Uh-uh, you go ahead," was the reply. (Had he recoiled a little from the knife? I wasn't sure.) "And I'll check out your form."

"Well, I'm not very good," said Malcolm, starting in by severing a leg.

After watching him seek out the joint between the drumstick and the thigh—he couldn't find it right away—David hollow-laughed and said, "I'd say you got *that* right!"

Later on, when the talk had turned to favorite bands and singers, Malcolm mentioned that he'd always been a big Paul Simon fan.

"Oh, gimme a break," said David. "I suppose you like Neil Diamond, too? And Barry Manilow, right?" He shook his head in great disgust, and kept on doing that every so often for the next few minutes, occasionally saying *"Paul Simon,"* just under his breath. Malcolm tried to look good-humored, and the rest of us acted as if David had to be just kidding around, making those absurd comparisons. And maybe he was. You simply couldn't tell with him.

When we'd almost polished off some pretty decent apple crisp that Allie'd made us for dessert, David suddenly put up his hand and said, "Who, other than my sister, wants to play a little tennis? Sometime. Like tomorrow afternoon, for instance. Any volunteers?"

There was a silence that stretched on too long.

"We-ell," I said, to break it, "I told you I don't *play*—I don't know how—but if—"

He cut me off. "What you're saying is, you'd really *like* to, but you can't," he said. "Right? You'd *love* to play with me, but lack the necessary skills."

"I guess," I said, suspicious once again. He had this way of *putting* things.

"So," he said. "Felicia *can't*. We'll have to sign her up for something else tomorrow afternoon. Let's see. What might a camper with her modest skills and, shall we say, *enthusiasms,* choose? I know! I've got a great idea. She *could* play hide-and-seek, inside the maze. And what's-his-name—*Paul Simon*—could play *with* her!" He looked across at Malcolm for the first time, and he laughed as if that was a private joke they shared.

"That way," he said, "if she gets lost or scared, she'd have someone who could come to save her, lickety-split." He looked at *me* and laughed this time.

"All right," said Allie. "Let's stop picking on Felicia. I'll play some tennis with you."

"You any good?" he asked.

"You'll see," she said. She smiled and winked at me.

"Okay, hotshot," David said, "I'll tell you what. I'll give

you thirty-love a game, and we can play a set for something."

"Oh?" said Al. "Like what?" I think I've mentioned Allie was an athlete; she positively thrived on competition.

"How about the loser has to tell the truth," he said, to my surprise, I must say, "in answer to a question chosen by the winner. *Or* she has to face a consequence—do something that he says."

" 'He' says?" she said. "You've got your pronouns wrong, good buddy. But even if you didn't, that's a sucker bet. The winner could tell the loser to . . . *I* don't know, do something really gross or dangerous."

"No, no," said David. "Nothing gross or dangerous. It'd be like when you're hypnotized, you know? They say you can't be made to do anything that goes against your morals, or might hurt you. This'd be like that. The consequence could never be a thing you wouldn't do if you were hypnotized. And you can say."

Allie shook her head. Not "no," but "this is weird."

"Okay," she said. "It's a bet, I guess. I'm not going to lose, but even if I did, I could always just answer the question."

"Truthfully," said David.

"Yeah, yeah, sure," she said. And with that, they shook—one of those jivemaster shakes that always loses me about step three, but they were both good athletes.

I had to give her credit. Much more than me, and much, much more than Malcolm, she had acted like herself with David, talking just the way she would with . . . *I* don't know, some kid at school she'd known for years, though maybe not that well. She'd also sure made Kate relax, I noticed. As we all got up to clear the table, she was smiling in a way that didn't look as if she had been ordered to, by terrorists, or something. I told myself that I was going to work a little harder on *my* attitude, starting . . . well, our first full day with David, which would be *tomorrow*.

As I had hoped, he didn't show for breakfast the next morning. That meant that none of us would see him till the afternoon, and then he had that tennis match with Allie on his schedule.

She took her car to school that day, and offered us a ride back "home," but Mal and I preferred to walk. And on the way, I raised the subject of our newfound "friend" again.

"I forgot to tell you that I saw him at the pool," I said. "He did the most amazing dive. But before that, he tried to make me think he was drowning. He sat on the bottom holding on to the drain, and gave me the finger."

"What?" said Malcolm. "When was that?"

"Yesterday," I said. "After Kate had talked to us. While you were home."

Mal had borrowed Allie's car—she always left the keys in it for him—and taken some dirty laundry to his house, where some successor to the storied Martha would take care of it. The only reason he didn't have his own car was that it was up at the Foreign Car Center, waiting for some part to get here from Bavaria, I guess. The only reason that his clothes did not get washed at Mycroft House was that I hadn't volunteered and he, I'm pretty sure, did not know how to run the washer and the dryer.

"He gave you the *finger*?" Malcolm said. "What did he do *that* for?"

"I don't know," I said. "For kicks, I guess. Or to be funny. I don't know why he does lots of things. But I didn't let on that I'd seen him. I pretended that I'd never gone to look down in the pool."

"He's a *jerk,*" said Malcolm, and he sounded totally unlike himself. "I can't *stand* him. I figure we owe Kate a few days of . . . whachacallit, *brother*-sitting, but then I'm getting out of here." We'd started walking up the driveway. "He's going to ruin everything. I was afraid this was too good to be true." He slipped an arm around my waist, but I could tell that he was angry, still. And something more than angry. I'd baby-sat for kids who'd say things in the tone of voice that he'd just used. Descriptive adjectives for them? Try "sulky"—yes, and "spoiled."

"Well, possibly he'll settle down as he gets used to us," I said. I wasn't ready to go home; I hadn't finished sipping from the well of life. "I just wish I knew what the real story was, about what happened where they lived before."

"You know," said Malcolm, "I do, too. In fact, I had a little chat with my old man about that yesterday. I asked him whether if I found out what town they came from, he couldn't get somebody down at the paper to look into it. *You* know—call up the editor of the paper out there, and ask him for the poop on David Mycroft. I'm pretty sure that Allie knows. What town they're from, I mean—I *think* in Indiana. I'm going to ask her."

Almost in spite of myself, I was a bit impressed by that. I'd never had what I would call "a little chat" with "my old man." And even if I ever did, he wouldn't have connections like the ones that Mr. Warren had. It seemed there wasn't much that Malcolm couldn't ask for, and (this was even more amazing) *get*. I *guess* I was "impressed" by that. Kind of. In a way.

"I guess they're playing tennis now," I said. An idea had

just occurred to me, a good one. "Al and David—I wonder if she'll beat him; bet she does. I'd almost like to watch them play, except . . ." I stopped and smiled at Mal.

"Except for what?" he said, on cue.

"Except I know this place we might enjoy a visit to." I pointed at the path that branched off to our right. "Down there."

"What *kind* of place?" said Malcolm.

I put my book bag down and spun away from him, to make my full skirt twirl around my legs. I dropped my eyes in phony modesty and put a fingertip against my lips.

"A kind of *special* place," I murmured huskily. "You'll see. A kind of little bower." And I looked up at him and smiled what I intended as a terribly seductive, only slightly comic, little smile.

He seemed to get the message.

"Well," he said. "A *bower,* eh?" I could tell from how he said it that he didn't know the meaning of the word. But he assumed that he might like . . . whatever it turned out to be. He also dropped his school stuff, and we started down the path.

He liked it at first sight. "Aha!" he said, when it came into view. And, reaching for my hand, he did what I imagine guys have done from Adam on: He led me toward the mattress. He didn't ask how come, or when I'd learned that it was there; he just let his genes (or hormones, is it?) do the talking. Me, too: I kicked my sandals off, along the way.

It was our first time on a (sort of) bed, and I would say that we adapted rather quickly. Before five minutes passed, our shirts were off, and with them my front-closing, lightweight bra. And just because (oh, sure) I knew my skirt would wrinkle terribly, I let him help me off with it, and then observed while he removed his baggy olive pants.

That put us way, way out there on the sea of life, I felt, sailing on the outer edge of my experience. Beyond that point, I knew, were the untasted pleasures of a whole new world, in addition to some dangerous reefs and currents.

It soon became quite obvious to me that Malcolm had assigned himself the role of captain on this voyage—and that, as such, he knew some ways to win the crew's cooperation.

"You are *so* beautiful," he murmured. "So beautiful . . . and beautiful . . . and beautiful." He made it clear, with kisses and with touches both, which parts of me he was referring to.

A little later on, and not to my surprise—in fact with my assistance—I could feel my briefs go sliding down my legs and off my feet. A further yank and wriggle meant that *both* of us were beautiful as flowers in the field, or similarly naked, anyway.

This circumstance was *very* nice, in my opinion, and broad daylight made it even nicer, yes. I felt wild and wicked and extremely worldly. And so happily involved in all that I was seeing, feeling, doing—yes, the here and now—that (for the first time) I was finding it "too good for words."

Malcolm, though, was murmuring again. "You on the Pill?" I heard him say. *Uh-oh.*

"No," I said. "Oh, *no*. I'm *not*." Because we'd never mentioned birth control before, I guess I'd thought it wouldn't come up then. Oh, yes, I was *extremely* callow, wasn't I?

"Well, look," he said. "I don't have a condom, but I'll be

really, really careful, promise. I won't . . . while I'm inside you—*you* know."

I sure *did* know. Even my *mother* knew what that was all about. She'd mentioned it to me (in what I'd call a semi-scream) at the end of a sentence that began "And *whatever* you do, don't *ever* let him . . ."

"Uh-uh," I said, and made a few deft moves to get my pelvic region out of . . . well, *harm's way*. "I'm sorry, but I absolutely *don't* without protection, not with anyone. But lookee here . . ."

Sometimes I amaze myself, and that was one such time. Though I'd been—foolishly—surprised by what had happened, I'd recovered close to perfectly. My *muse* and I had, anyway—I give her credit for that sentence, that sophisticated "no." The "lookee here" part was a different matter; it reflected something that I'd learned myself, while baby-sitting: When you take away the lovely crystal vase, you'd better substitute a real fun toy. So, though our voyage was shortly over, I could say "so be it" and not fret. What I felt was more adult, and much more sure of certain things.

One thing I was sure of was that Malcolm wasn't going to be the one I'd (one day) do it with—that it'd be a different kind of boy. A boy with more awareness of the way it felt to have a woman's body, wear a woman's shoes. And, secondly, that though I might be *ready* now (in one sense of the word), and unafraid, there wasn't any tearing hurry.

We were barely *starting* to reclothe ourselves when I heard someone whistling, and then stop whistling.

"Quick," I said to Malcolm, pulling on my skirt and diving in my top, and sitting straight up on the middle of the mattress with my bra stuffed under me. Luckily, his shirt

did not require buttoning, and his trousers didn't need a belt; he dropped down on the floor beside the mattress.

Seconds later, a twig snapped behind the bower's single wall, and then came David's head around the end of it. He closed one eye and put his hand up by the other, pretending that he had a camera.

"Click-click," he said. Or, make that *chortled*. "Gotcha-gotcha-*gotcha,* trespassers!" He walked out on the stones that still were not a terrace. He wore a blue bandana as a headband, keeping his blond hair in place, but otherwise was all in white, his tennis outfit. He clearly *had* been sweating.

"I saw your book bags by the road," he teased, cocking his head and whittling one forefinger with the other. "*I* was on my bike and heading into town to celebrate my victory—with, possibly, a double root beer float. But then I saw those book bags, and I thought: So, what's all *this?*" He stepped back a little, giving us the once-over. He stroked his chin. And then began to grin.

"If I had *really* brought my camera," he said, "and gotten here perhaps ten minutes earlier, I bet I would have had a shot I could have sold to *some*body. Eh, Fleesh?" He leered at me.

Malcolm tried to get above it all.

"What's he babbling about?" he said to me.

"I can't imagine," I replied.

David laughed. "Could you imagine putting on a T-shirt inside out?" he asked. "If, for instance, you were in a tearing hurry? Could you imagine *that*?"

I had on a simple, oversized striped T, with a nice rounded neckline that made it a cinch to get on and off, and which, given the fabric it was made of, was pretty near reversible—except, of course, it wasn't. You could tell from looking at the seams—as I did then—which way was right side out. I felt myself begin to blush.

"I must have had it on like this all day," I said defiantly.

"Yeah, *sure* you did," said David, and he became all serious and mock-severe. "I'm *ashamed* of you, Felicia; I really am. And, don't look now, but I believe you've hatched some *lan-dgeray*!"

And then he winked at me, before he turned away and started whistling again, as he went down the path. The song was "Mrs. Robinson"; that figured. And, yes, there was a bra strap, peeking out from underneath my fanny.

That was Monday afternoon. During dinner Monday night David gave some further meaning to the word *obnoxious*.

First on his agenda was the tennis match, the score of which was seven games to five, his favor. Allie, in her own defense, claimed the match was even closer than the score suggested. She said that of the seven games she lost, all but one had gone to deuce, including three when he'd been serving.

"Let's face it, buddy," she maintained, "if we played twice a week all summer, I'd be beating you before October came around. Even with no handicap."

"The *point* is that you didn't win today," said David. "Even with a handicap of half a game, each game, you didn't win. So, what that means is: I *am* the king. *I* rule the court, and *you're* my handmaid. My forehand- and my backhandmaid. And, although the game is over, you must keep on serving me—for I assume you'll choose the consequence. The truth could be a lot more painful, couldn't it?"

"So, what about the bet?" I said to Al. "You gonna pay him?"

"*Of course* she is," said David, not giving her a chance to answer. "We're . . . negotiating still. I'm trying to be reasonable, think up a consequence that wouldn't be too hard on her. She's probably exhausted, even though *I* hardly broke a sweat. I had to ride my bike to get a workout, after. And, speaking of *workouts* . . ." He turned toward his sister. "I think that *you* should know that Fleesh has secretly been doing some with Malcolm, here."

"Look," Kate said to him. She sounded really angry this time, totally fed up. "*How about you damn well cut this out?* You don't *have to* act this way. So, just stop *bugging* everyone, all right?" I'd never heard that tone from her before.

"Hey, don't jump on *me,*" he said. "*I'm* just making conversation. Telling everyone about my day. Isn't that what people do at din—?"

She cut him off. "I said *'All right?'* " she said. "Now *do* it! Just stop being such a *bug*!"

There was one of those repulsive silences again, which Allie finally broke by saying *she* was going to have some coffee with dessert, that David had been right, and she could use a pick-me-up.

After that, he acted less obnoxious, more like all the rest of us. When Kate asked if anyone wanted to play croquet, when we had finished dinner clean-up, he volunteered to get the mallets and the balls. And everybody said they'd play.

The game was uneventful for the longest time. Malcolm won, but David would've—he was clearly the best player—if he hadn't tried so many shots that bordered on impossible, and then done something . . . unexpected (you might say).

That happened when the game was almost over. Malcolm was ahead, but not by much, with the other three in hot pursuit, then me as the caboose. It was David's turn. He passed through a wicket, meaning he could take another shot. Now he had a choice. Malcolm's ball was over twenty feet in front of him, and in position for the last two wickets. He could try to make the real long shot and hit that ball, or turn around and aim at Kate's, a scant six feet behind him. Strategically, that was the better choice: he *should* hit Kate, then take the two shot bonus that he got and go get Malcolm. And it appeared that that was what he had in mind. He aimed at Kate, and hit her blue ball squarely.

Then came the unexpected.

"Well, well," he said. And then he went, picked up his ball, placed it next to Kate's, and put his foot on it. Instead of getting Malcolm, instead of *winning* . . . it seemed that he had something else in mind.

Grinning . . . well, *maniacally,* he took the hugest double-handed swing I'd ever seen. If he'd missed his ball and hit his foot, the way I might have done, he would have broken every bone in it, I'm sure.

But he didn't miss his ball.

There was a *thwack!* and Kate's ball was a streak of blue, rocketing across the lawn, and off the croquet field, and down a slope and on and on, still going fast until it disappeared into a flower bed. David's own red ball squirted out from underneath his foot from the force of the blow and rolled about three feet, which meant he'd forfeited his other shot—and now would absolutely, *surely* lose the game.

I switched my eyes to David's face as soon as I saw Kate's ball disappear. What I saw on it was deep, delicious satisfaction, pleasure at its zenith. And his expression didn't seem to change, even after Malcolm passed the last two wickets, hit the stake, and won the game.

While that was going on, I stole a look at Kate. She'd turned away and started going to retrieve her ball. She looked as if she'd shrunk; her head was down, her shoulders drooped. She seemed totally defeated.

David's mood continued to be quite the opposite. "Nice going, Mal," he said, completely cheerfully. And then he turned to Allie and, still sounding quite a bit more charming than he ever had before, said, "Now, let's you and me go talk about that consequence. . . ."

As they strolled away, I saw he even had her laughing.

Thirteen

I *ran* upstairs, up to my room, that night. I'd decided that there wasn't any time to lose. Even though I had some stuff to read for history, and physics problems to do, my novella had to take priority. And not because of Writing Workshop; it didn't even meet, next day.

No, my motivation came from . . . *history* is what I almost said. I knew that, once again, I was reacting and behaving loonily, but I found I couldn't help myself. I was worried after seeing Allison and David walking off the croquet lawn the way they did, almost like *friends*. As you know, some things that I'd put down in my novella had, for sure, then happened in real life, and always to the corresponding characters. So what I felt I had to do, at once, was speedily reverse the action in that Dermott-Annabel relationship—break them up before they went beyond that first, exploratory kiss.

A part of me did actually pooh-pooh the whole idea of doing that, I must insist. Allison (I *knew*) was not about to get involved with David. He was too odd for *anyone*. Sure, Allie was a true adventuress, but even she would not cross certain borders, boundary lines—like into Nutcase City. But still, I wasn't going to take the chance.

I was in such a hurry that I didn't even bother with an outline. I didn't really need one, anyway. I knew where I was going and I went, full speed. As follows:

10

Annabel D. Day could not have been more pleased. Her mouth-to-mouth was working very well, no doubt about it. Not only was her patient showing signs of life by wiggling his tongue (delightfully), but also he was proving he had normal range of motion in his arms and, most especially, his hands. Indeed, once he'd reestablished that she was a well-proportioned human female, dressed in not too many lightweight clothes, he seemed to get the urge to move her from behind his chair to someplace where he'd get to know her easier and better—like, say, straddling his lap.

And Annabel, enjoying, was cooperating when—and suddenly—the door behind them opened with a crash!

Annabel's wet mouth abandoned Dermott's fast, and her alert blue eyes snapped open. Standing in the doorway were two figures. One, the big dog Grace, looked pleased and wagged her tail. The other one did not: Marge Costner.

"Well, I'll be damned," said Marge.

Dermott Costner struggled to his feet, sweeping Annabel aside as if she were a beaded curtain. But what he said seemed almost worse, to her.

"It's not what you are thinking, sweetie. Really," Dermott said to Marge.

"Don't 'sweetie' me," she sneered. "Get out of here. Go sweep the castle keep, or swab the Great Hall's walls. Work off a little of that extra energy you seem to have. I'll see *you* later, Mr. Mud."

"Sure," he said. "Of course. But let me say: I'd never seen this girl before. She just came in and started—"

"Go!" Marge ordered him. Her right arm rose up, ramrod straight, and pointed at the door. He went.

"Now," she said to Annabel. "Let's hear *your* side of it."

"Well," she said, still fighting for composure, "your stepson found me here, admiring his painting. He told me all about himself, and Adeline, and I felt *sorry* for him, so I—"

"Wait," commanded Marge. "My *stepson,* did you say? '*His* painting'?"

"Why, yes," said Annabel. "He told me how you got him into treatment, where he learned to paint, and how—"

"Time *out,*" snapped Marge, emphatically. "It sounds like you've been fed a line of bull so thick and rich that it'd fertilize three-quarters of the state of South Dakota. That bozo's not my stepson. His name is Dermott Pugh, and I'll bet a dollar that the only thing he's ever painted is the hull of the USS *Boysie*"—A.D. later figured out that what she'd heard was *Boise*—"on which he was an ordinary seaman not that long ago."

"What?" said Annabel. "You mean . . . ?"

"I mean," she said, "that Dermott is, like you, someone who came for sanctuary. You didn't think I only put my notices in high-school girls' rooms, did you? He was caller number one—the first one who was *serious*, that is. He's been here for a month. I'm sure he's a deserter in the Navy's books, by now."

"And the painting . . . ?" Annabel gestured toward that hideosity.

"Mine, of course," said Marge. "*Prophylactic Over Plastic*. Just back from the Whitney Biennial."

"So—the *groaning* . . . ?" A.D. blurted out, before she'd thought to think.

"Groaning?" Marge looked puzzled for an instant.

"Yes," said Annabel, deciding that she might as well press on and try to find out everything. "The groaning sounds that Dermott said he made while he was working. Last night we heard them—after two it was. They came from here."

"Oh, *them*," said Marge. She dropped her eyes, but more in modest pleasure than embarrassment, thought Annabel. "While he was *working*, eh? That's right, he did come by. Dermott has his faults, but like a lot of sailors, when it comes to pleasure cruises, well . . . Those sounds, they came from him or me, or maybe *us*, depending when you heard them. Surely''—and her eyes came up to Annabel's—''you know whereof I speak.''

''Oh, yes,'' said Annabel, now badly flustered. ''Good golly, I'm so solly—*sorry*. I was way, way out of bounds on this, and—''

''Don't apologize,'' said Marge, and she was smiling. ''I quite understand. At your age, I'd have done the same. But you're a pretty girl. I'm sure you're old enough to have your own library card, and I'm equally certain you can find your own writhing material (if you know what I mean), without any help from me. Such as that handsome Martin Silverado.'' And she smacked her lips. ''Anyway, shouldn't you be either still or back in school?''

''Yes, certainly. Oh, absolutely, yes,'' said Annabel. ''I can't believe he lied to me, like that. But still, it's all my stupid fault. From now on, I promise you, I'll stay in my own wing and never, ever give the time of day to—''

''Shoo,'' said Marge. She made a sweeping motion with one hand. ''Get out of here, yourself, go on. And if you hear a little groaning going on tonight''—she winked—''you'll know our Dermott's learning how to be a better sanctuarian, that's all.'' And then she chuckled.

Annabel D. Day went out the door and down the stairs and back to school, post haste. What a *dork* that Dermott Costner—*Pugh*—had been revealed to be.

And then she started laughing, at herself—how gullible she'd been. Now, she thought, she *might* fall back on Martin Silverado, and that picture—Martin stretched out on a bed, herself collapsing backward onto him—made her laugh some more. Hell, she thought, why not take a shot at something better, like that handsome Lansing Pine, the banker's son, who'd soon be coming home from Yale.

There, I thought, when I had finished writing that; *there, that ought to do it.* I was now completely off the hook, with little time to spare. And if Allie reconsidered and decided she might like to do some stuff with Malcolm (Martin) after all—well, I could live with that.

Oh, I still *liked* him, plenty, and we had had fun. And knowing him *had* been a growth experience for me, no doubt about it. But, in fairness, she had been the one who brought him to the house, to start with. And, much as I was drawn to many of his qualities and . . . aspects (such as his money, manners, looks, clothes, body, and techniques), there were other areas in which he looked as if he might turn out to be a little disappointing.

If your mouth fell open, reading that, and if you thought, This girl should have her head examined, I don't blame you. After all, when you put money, manners, looks, clothes, body, and techniques (I didn't even mention *car*) on one side of an equation, and then the "is less than" sign, what on earth could you reasonably put on the other?

(Mother? Do I see your hand up? *What,* then?

Oh, I see. *You* think I ought to have my head examined, too.)

Well, maybe it's the writer in me, but . . . well, how

about *respect*? Respect not only for my points of view and my opinions, but also for my wants and needs and talents. For who I am and what I might become. *For my best interests.* Even when they might conflict with his desires.

And how about compassion? Sensitivity? Honesty and openness? I'll tell you something funny—not ha-ha but strange. Now that I feel more *experienced,* which is to say more self-assured and valuable, I find I'm more inclined to say (to *dare* to say) that I insist a "boyfriend" have those qualities.

If you're thinking this is almost like a classic switcheroo, in which in this case I (the girl), having finally gotten *him* (the boy) in bed with all his clothes off, now decide that I don't really think he's all that wonderful . . . if you're thinking *that,* that isn't really right. I honestly believe that all along I've had some reservations, that I hadn't made a deep commitment to this boy. And that, on top of *that,* the more I saw Mal in . . . oh, different situations, the more I saw he was . . . oh, different ways I wasn't all that fond of. That he was maybe just a little immature—or maybe what I really mean is *spoiled.*

But don't misunderstand. This doesn't mean I'm looking for *perfection*—not at all. I know it isn't out there. A writer has to face that fact; all characters, if they are true to life, are good *and* bad, up and down, true and false, brainy and *estúpido.* All I'm trying to say is a boy (girl, too) should show he/she is *trying*—to be caring, giving, understanding, truthful. And that I'm not totally convinced that that's the case with Malcolm Warren. I'm not sure he thinks he *has to* try. That's all I'm really saying. So, let's get on to something else.

Like whether what I'd written, there in Chapter Ten, was any good—or good enough—as *writing.* Although

I'd read it over twice, and made some minor changes, I wasn't feeling totally secure. Had I strained, too much, my story's credibility? Would a woman like Marge Costner—single, late-thirtyish, successful, and attractive—even *bother* to have an affair with an early-twenties sailor? Hmm, I thought—what *bother*? It didn't mean she couldn't/wouldn't *also* date successful men of her own age. I mean, I couldn't see my *mother* taking in a Dermott, but so what? Marge Costner kept old shriveled carrots in the crisper.

And then another thought exploded in my mind. Was it possible, I asked myself, that David "Mycroft" wasn't anybody's brother? "Anybody" meaning Kate, of course. Might he be, instead, another Dermott "Costner," a young *lover*? One who Kate was maybe getting tired of, and wanted to ease out of their relationship? Were Allie and myself *alternatives* that she was pushing out in front of him, or maybe even sort of *decoys,* possibly, who over time would introduce him to the larger flock of local high-school "chicks"? Or, might it be the other way, that David recently had gotten sick of *her*?

These were fascinating possibilities, I thought. David was obviously still playing along with this brother-sister fiction (if that's what it was), but he could also be threatening her, maybe even *blackmailing* her, saying he would turn *her* name to mud, in town, unless she gave him money, or a car, or something. The picture of him knocking her croquet ball far across the lawn was printed in my mind, indelibly. It *couldn't* be an isolated incident, a small part of one game. It was, beyond a doubt, *symbolic,* I was sure. Allison and Malcolm weren't writers; it's possible they hadn't realized that. But I sure had. And passion of the sort he had displayed most often would occur between two people who were . . . what? I leave that up to you.

It was getting really late but, operating under the spell of that kind of thinking (I suppose), plus all the stuff I'd thought concerning Malcolm recently, I decided to postpone the physics and the history a little longer and toss off another fun-filled part of Chapter Ten.

I won't make you read it, but . . . the sound of Fiona's oboe practicing (that afternoon) in a cozy tower room high up in Costner's Castle, so inflamed young Martin Silverado that he tiptoed through the halls and up the narrow stairs to get as close as possible to . . . well, the *source* of those seductive sounds. Thus, after she'd finished with her practicing, she found him just outside her door, standing on the landing, reaching out for her, adoringly. With a smile, she led him back into the room, which had a mattress on the floor; inside her oboe case there also was a condom, just in case. But, instead of using it, she scurried out the door and locked it after her. And then went down the staircase, laughing, accompanied by Grace, the dog, who (it turned out) had quite a taste for music. All of them knew the maid would let him out, eventually. . . .

Oh, yes, I fell asleep before I ever got to history or physics.

Fourteen

I think I've mentioned that it doesn't take me long to fall asleep, and that once I'm in the arms of Morpheus, I'm apt to stay there for a while. Sleep is something I enjoy; I'm glad that they invented beds. The first and last things that we do in them (get born and die) may not be memorable, but think how glad we are for all the in-betweens.

I also am a dreamer who remembers dreams. I keep hoping for some hot material that I can use in stories (or a revelation of some sort, perhaps concerning afterlife), but by and large my dreams are neither as erotic nor as informational as I would like. Typically, they have to do with small anxieties, or nonsense; I never seem to slay the dragon, cross the Rubicon, or win a prize for anything.

The one I had that night began quite ordinarily. I was in a corridor at school—or at *a* school, I should say; it wasn't Northfield High. The halls were wider and more crowded, and the doors to all the rooms were made, in part, of frosted glass, instead of clear. In lieu of numbers on their surfaces, the doors had words on them, explaining what the room was used for, such as "Sophomore English," "Physics Lab," and "Pipe Dreams/Lost and Found."

What I was doing in the corridor was trying to catch up with Malcolm Warren. But I couldn't. If I went faster, so did he, and he was much too far ahead of me to hear me call his name. It almost seemed we were connected by a beam consisting of repellent particles, which nobody could see, and no one else could feel.

But then, and suddenly, Malcolm opened one of the doors and disappeared into the room behind it. Following, I felt relieved; now I'd catch up with him. But when I got to the door, I stopped. Written on it were the words "Girls' Shower Room—No Boys Allowed Except for Malcolm." From inside, I heard a laugh and squeal of pleasure, the sorts of sounds a girl will make sometimes, when she is being tickled.

Instead of reaching for the doorknob, I woke up.

You know the way you come awake sometimes and lie there, motionless, just *listening,* real hard? That's what I did then. I had no idea what I would hear, but still I listened for it.

When the sound came, it was from outside, and wafted in

my open window; it was also unmistakable: a splash. I thought some animal or person had jumped into (fallen in) the pool. Tossing back the covers, I got out of bed and staggered window-ward.

As I've explained, I think, my room was on the second floor, in back, which meant I had an unobstructed view of everything behind the house: the hedges and the gardens and the pool—and, farther on, the maze. Or, at least I did when it was day, or there was moonlight, as there was that night, moonlight even brighter than three nights before, when I'd been in the maze.

So, despite my slight astigmatism, the scene below was pretty clear to me. The first thing/person that I saw was Allison, sort of skipping sideways—but not fast—along the edge of the pool, and looking down into it. She had her hands together near her chin, and her elbows pressed against her ribs, below her breasts, as if she was a little cold. And possibly she was; she was wearing what my mother might have called her "birthday suit."

That, in and of itself, was an arresting sight. Allison has lovely clothes and wears them well, but she is even better-looking naked. She doesn't have an ounce of excess flab on her, nor is she in the least bit scrawny; in other words, the parts that *should* be are both round and firm, and elsewhere she is flat, or long and lean, with muscle definition. A lot of people I could name are jealous of her body.

But almost surely not the person who then surfaced in the pool, the one who she'd been looking for, the one who, chances are, had made the splash that got me out of bed. *Appreciative,* he'd be, but *jealous,* no. Oh, yes, it was a "he," all right. Not Lansing Pine, or Dermott Pugh, or even Malcolm Warren. *David.*

I gaped; he took two strokes and put his hands up on the deck beside the pool. He ducked his head and tossed it back so that his long blond hair ran down his back; then, with no apparent effort, he pulled himself out of the water. He was just as nude as Allie was, and every bit as gorgeous.

Of course he started chasing her around the pool; guys always do. In the moonlight, they both looked like marble statues, brought to life. She reached the other side and then dove in, heading straight across the width; he followed suit. She didn't surface till she reached the side, then she, too, came out fast and easily, pulling herself forward on her stomach.

But just when it appeared she would escape, he literally *erupted* from the water, right behind her, and reaching, grabbed her by the ankle. An instant later, he was also lying on the deck, and she was trying to roll away from him, and laughing.

He kept his grip, then moved it up her legs and to her waist; he slithered on the wet concrete till he was right beside her. By then, he'd got his arms around her back, and she had seized his head and brought it closer to her mouth. She threw a smooth long leg across his thigh.

I stepped back from the window (can you stand this?), *blushing*.

Would I have *liked* to watch whatever happened next? You want the truth? Okay. Well, yes (the answer is). It was exciting; they were beautiful. And also, I believe it almost is a writer's *duty* to observe—whatever she can see. Everything's "material," let's face it.

But still, I didn't watch. One of them was Allie, my good friend, and I believe that friends give other friends not only privacy but, yes, *respect*. I want it, so I have to give it, too.

And watching any more than what I'd seen would not be—so it seemed to me—respectful. *Interesting,* perhaps *informative,* but not respectful.

I got back into bed and lay there.

Of course I couldn't help but listen—and *conclude*. The listening, thank God (I guess), was not . . . enlightening. I thought I heard some splashes later on, but that was all. The concluding didn't go much better.

My best *guess* was that I had not been looking at a first. I couldn't *know* that, naturally, but the impression that I'd gotten, watching them, was of two people who were . . . well, *familiar* with each other. And, thinking back, I realized that cagey Allie, ever since the first time that she'd mentioned David (and dismissed him, seemingly), had always sounded *tolerant* of him, at least.

Of course I then thought of my story, of Annabel and Dermott Pugh. Which couple was the chicken and which one the egg? Would something happen now to split up Al and David?

I finally went back to sleep, still wondering.

In the morning, I awakened with my mind made up. I was Allie's friend; as such, I had a further role to play. A friend who knows her friend is doing something risky, like abusing drugs or alcohol, is duty-bound to intervene. David was attractive in the same way those things were; he was also sort of out of bounds and slightly wicked, and appeared to be equipped to change one's consciousness. But he was dangerous, too, I thought. Not in the sense of being, like, a murderer, or something, but because he was . . . unstable. I didn't know if he was (as the saying goes) "too much," in the sense of being way too wild, turned up too high, or "not enough," meaning that he hadn't fully recovered from his accident and so was running (as they also say) on less than a full charge. But, in either case, I didn't like knowing that Allie was involved with him. She had a little wild streak, too; that made him, in my mind, all the more unsuitable for her.

So, first thing in the morning, I got dressed in haste, and then went down the hall and waited in her room, as soon as I had heard her leave it for the bathroom.

"Hey, early bird," she said, when she returned. I was sitting primly on her bed. She had a printed silk kimono on, and didn't look the least bit sleep-deprived. "What's up?"

"I saw somebody chasing you around the pool last night," I blurted out. I'm so subtle and oblique, so diplomatic. "The splashing woke me up. I was afraid an animal had fallen in, so I got up and looked. But when I saw it was you two, I went straight back to bed." Not knowing where to look, and embarrassed to the core, I kept my eyes fixed on her face, almost daring her to tell me that I'd dreamed it.

Allie smiled a little rueful smile and ran a hand along her pixie haircut.

"I was afraid of that," she said. "But then I thought, you sleep real soundly, and I told him that we couldn't make a lot of noise. That was his consequence, of course—that we'd go skinny-dipping in the moonlight."

"Uh-huh," I said, and also smiled. "I got the feeling that the two of you were . . . That this wasn't, like, the first time that you'd—"

"You got the feeling I've been making out with David," Allie interrupted. "And you're right." She shook her head and turned away from me, shrugging off her robe. She had on pale blue string-bikini briefs. "I guess it was a crazy thing to do. But—I don't know—my parents were away, I'd moved down here, it all seemed sort of dreamlike—where I could go ahead and do, oh, *anything,* without there being any consequences." She went and got a soft tan chamois shirt from off a hanger, and turned to face me as she put it on. "That first day, when I saw him in those little-bitty swimming trunks, I guess I just went . . ." She shook her head and smiled again and made a sound like *"Ghlomph!"* the sound a shark might make, perhaps, while scarfing down a swimmer.

"I understand," I said. "I really do." And the amazing thing was that I really did. "But still I can't help worrying. The guy . . ."

She'd raised a hand to shut me up. "It's over with," she said. "Last night was the finale. Promise you. I've promised *me,* already. I've had my fun and so has he, but now it's over. We never said we were in *love,* or anything like that. It was just—*you* know—a little thing. A *fling.*"

I nodded, thinking that I *did* know, actually. Two weeks ago, I would have known the words, but not the music—the overture that went before the action. Now, I thought, I did. Not that I was poised to do what *she* had done, you understand.

"Besides," she said. She pulled on corduroys and sat down on the bed, not far from me. "I wouldn't want to get involved in what he's going through." Leaning forward, she picked up her socks.

"You mean, like, from the accident?" I said. "His having to relearn a lot of basic stuff?" I had to grin. "*Some* basic stuff?"

She shook her head. "No, not exactly." She took a breath, then blew it out her nose. "The thing is that he's got a very different story than the one we heard from Kate.

About the accident, I mean. I haven't decided whether I believe him or not. It's sort of . . . *I* don't know, far out. Like a true-life-story movie on TV."

She didn't get right into it, however.

"Well, *what?*" I said. "You're going to tell me, aren't you?" It wasn't hard to get my interest in a *story,* right?

"I guess," she said, and shook her head again, as if to say I-know-this-is-ridiculous-but-still.

"David says he had a passenger the night he had the accident," she said. "A girl. And she was killed."

"My God," I said. "You're *kidding.*" Of course I thought of Dermott and his Adeline. But I had made that up. "So he *does* remember stuff from then—the accident."

"Not exactly," Allie said. "I'll get to that. What he says is that the car went off some little bridge and landed in a river, like with Senator Kennedy that time. Except *he* managed to get himself and the girl out of the car—that *is* the way he cut his wrists, by the way—and he even pulled her right up on the bank."

"That was when he realized she was dead?" I said. I wanted to be clear on every detail. "When he got her out of the water?"

"Something like that, I guess," said Al. She'd pushed her feet into a pair of clogs and now was sitting there, just looking at the rug, her hands spread on her knees. "The extra-weird part is that now he can't remember picking up a girl, the accident itself, or escaping from the car—all that's a total blank."

"Huh?" I said. "So, where'd he find it out from?"

"Kate," said Allie. "She told him that he came into her room, still soaking wet, at two A.M. His wrists were bleeding; he was in a state of shock, she said. But he told her what had happened; apparently, he *did* remember then." She took a peek at me, and then went back to looking at the floor. "Well, she bandaged him up and put him to bed, and then got in her car and drove to where he'd said, and found the girl and, well, *disposed of her.*" She didn't look at me this time.

"*Kate* did that?" I said. "Kate *Mycroft?*" And I shook my head. "That's unbelievable. That doesn't sound like her at all."

"Just wait," said Al. "There's more." She hitched around and got a bent leg on the bed. She looked directly at me now. "According to David, when Kate got back to the house, she woke him up and told him what she'd done. She said she'd done it to protect him from an ugly mess, a scandal—and probably a lawsuit and a trial. She said that now she had to call the cops, report the accident. After all, his car *was* wrecked and in the river. She also told him what *he* had to tell the cops when they arrived—that he'd driven off the bridge and gotten hurt escaping from the car, and somehow walked back home, passing out a time or two along the way."

"In other words," I said, to help her out, "she told him just to tell the truth, except leave out the girl. Or so he *said* she did."

"I guess," said Allie. "And he said that wasn't hard for him to do, seeing as by then he didn't remember anything about a girl at all."

"Hmm," I said. I closed my eyes and pinched my nose, trying to think this all through clearly, like Hercule Poirot, the great detective. It seemed he claimed he'd had—still had—delayed amnesia. Was there such a thing? I didn't know. "But how about the next day, when a girl was *missing*? Someone David *knew,* maybe even someone he'd been seen with, somewhere, that same night?"

"I wondered that exact same thing," said Allie. "But David told me Kate told *him* she hadn't recognized the girl, and that she'd looked more like a 'city girl,' which was Kate's nice way of saying 'little slut.' David said that was quite possible. Apparently, he used to cruise around a lot—he had a real nice car, a Porsche—and pick up girls at different places, drive-ins and like that. He didn't come right out and say he picked them up for sex, but, well . . ." She shrugged and made a face. "He told me *that* part just last night."

I nodded sympathetically. All of that seemed pretty David-ish, to me.

"So, now," I said, still trying to figure out what-all was going on at present, in the here and now, "he's worried that he got his sister into this? That they might find the body and connect her to it somehow?" But those sorts of concerns didn't seem to jibe with all the interactions that I'd seen between the two of them, particularly that bit with the croquet ball.

"Not exactly," Allie said. "There's one last thing I didn't tell you yet. According to David, sister Kate is doing a real number on him now. She's threatening to turn him in—tell the cops about the girl and show them where *he* hid the body—unless he gives her half of the money that their parents left him."

"Wait, wait," I said. "Hold on. Kate's parents are alive and well in Scottsdale, Arizona, and—" I stopped that sentence in midflight, as Allie raised her eyebrows. "Or so she said."

"*He* says that's utter bullshit," Allie said. "He says their parents died of different kinds of cancer, back in 'ninety-one—within three months of each other. He says he really, really loved them, a whole lot. He and Kate inherited a pile, a half to each of them."

"And now she wants three-quarters," I said slowly. "I suppose that's possible. *She* bought the Grunfeld place, and so on. And when it comes to money, people never seem to have enough." I ran the story through my mind again. "She certainly would be a whole lot more believable than he'd be, to the cops or in a courtroom, say." I was already seeing this climactic scene, in pictures, on TV. "She seems completely straight, and he's a veritable spaceman."

The thing about all this was . . . you couldn't flatly say *"Impossible"* to any of it. Oh, it was most *unlikely,* sure. But that didn't make it fiction, necessarily. Things like this *did* happen, and probably no one ever thought they'd happen to *them,* or to anyone they knew. But they did keep happening, to *someone.*

"There's just one thing that I don't understand," said Al. "Why *us*? You know what I mean? Why did Kate invite *us* here? You'd think she'd want to keep him isolated, sort of, wouldn't you? And just keep messing with his mind, working on his fear of being thrown in jail, or something. I mean, she wouldn't want him telling anyone his side of it, I wouldn't think."

Of course. I got a little angry that I hadn't thought of that, myself. Why us, indeed? It didn't seem to make good sense for Kate to ask us there, assuming that his story was the truth.

I looked down at my watch. I needed time to think.

"Boy, I don't know," I said. "But I know *this.*" I jumped up off the bed. "Even if you drive, we may be late to school. And me, I can't face physics on an empty stomach." I started for the door.

“I’m really glad you brought this up,” said Allie. “I’m going to need some help deciding what to do—if anything.” She picked her book bag off the floor.

“Sure, of course,” I said. “Let’s talk some more when we get home. And Mal might be a help, you know? He’s asked his dad to try to find out more about the Mycrofts. He wouldn’t have to know . . . well, anything, except what David told you.”

“Yeah,” said Allie. We were going down the stairs. “Right now, I’m feeling slightly idiotic for—*you* know. He didn’t seem to be the sort who’d have to . . . look for girls, like that.”

“I guess it’s hard to tell about a boy,” I said.

I could almost hear my mother say, “I’ll drink to that.”

Fifteen

Malcolm wasn't with us when we reconvened in Allie's room that afternoon. He'd had to stay in school—I think it was a meeting of the flying club—but said he'd join us later. I sort of got the feeling that the subject of *our* meeting—namely and to wit: Another Version of the David Mycroft Story—wasn't all that big a grabber to the guy. He even treated us to one of those huge sighs that people use in place of "How much longer must I listen to this kind of crap?" or "Someone less polite than me would tell you to . . . oh, never mind."

"I think we ought to talk with Kate," I said to Al. Ever the good guest, I'd flopped down on her bed, but at the foot of it, so she could have the pillow.

"Oof," said Allie. "Tell her everything that David said to me? That little bro's accusing her of blackmail?"

"Yeah," I said. "I think we've almost *got to*. Even though *of course* we'd rather not. The good part is that, chances are, the whole entire story is a crock, and she can even *prove* it is—call her parents up and let us speak to them would be a way, I guess. But there *is* that one chance in a guhzillion David's telling you the truth. And if he is . . ." I shrugged. "Basically, I'd like to see what her *reaction* is."

"Um. I *guess* that we could tell her," Allie said. "I mean, I guess we *should*. It's obvious there's *something* going on. Like at the croquet game. He gave that ball of hers a *wallop*, didn't he?"

"Gleefully," I said. "That wasn't ordinary brother-sister stuff. You'd think with all the difference in their ages, they'd be much more . . . *mellow—I* don't know. When he was born, she must have been in college, just about."

"One thing I was wondering," said Al. "Suppose his story's true? Or let's say we *think* it is. What do we do then?"

"I don't know," I said again. "I suppose at some point we'd decide to drag our parents in. Actually, I was sort of hoping, if it came to that, that we could tell *your* parents first." Allie started looking pained. "Seeing as you *met* Kate through your mother," I concluded, as if I had no other reason for suggesting that.

"I guess you're right," said Allison, my reasonable friend. She smiled. "It's not the sort of situation that your mom would welcome having you mixed up in, is it? A boy, a girl killed in an accident, and blackmail?"

"No, not really," I said, grinning back at her. "Come to think of it"—I scratched my head and made a face—"it's *possible* that I forgot to mention there were *boys* at Mycroft House, at all."

When Malcolm joined us, not quite sixty minutes later, he was clearly not in all that great a mood. His eyes went once around the room, first taking in the two of us, relaxing on the bed, then seeing both the chairs piled high with Allie's clothes. He sank down on the floor, his back against the wall, knees up.

"So, what's dear David shoveled out to someone now?" he asked.

Allison and I regarded each other. I made a little gesture toward her with one hand.

"Okay," she said, and looked away from me and down at Malcolm. "This is what he told me."

Having had some practice telling it to me, she got the story out coherently and clearly. Hearing it that way, from start to finish, I found myself believing it was definitely *possible,* though not exactly likely. But, watching Malcolm as she spoke, I realized he wasn't buying any part of it, at all. When she finished, he sat there with an expression on his face I'd seen before.

I'd had a math teacher in seventh grade, a Mr. Cone, who used to look at kids like that sometimes, before he spoke, before he made some comment on the answer they'd just given. It was a look that said: That was probably the stupidest thing I've heard, from anyone, in my entire life. Mr. Cone had gone away to teach at some boarding school in Vermont the year after I had him, but Malcolm brought him back into my mind as if I'd seen him yesterday.

"David Mycroft is a total 'hole," said Mal. "A complete and utter one. This is just so typical of him, it makes me want to puke." He sighed.

"Can't you see what wavy-Davy's trying to do?" He aimed that straight at Allison. "He wants to get you feeling so damn sorry for him that you think the very *least* that you can do is bounce him on your Beautyrest a time or two."

Whoo-ee, I thought; what's going on? Dr. Sigmund Warren giving his analysis? It wasn't like the *Malcolm* Warren that I knew to talk that way. Or was it? Was he simply feeling *threatened* by this David? Worried that he might be losing his position as bull elephant (to cows like Al and me)? (What was Jung's first name? *Felicia,* was it?) Mal would absolutely turn to *coleslaw* (it occurred to me) if ever he found out what Allie had been doing with the guy for days and days. Bounce him on her Beautyrest, indeed!

Allison, of course, did not take kindly to . . . well, having him imply that he could read another person's strategies and motivations—particularly a boy's—more easily than she could. Or that anyone could ever *trick* her into bed.

She put her disagreement bluntly.

"Bull," she said. "You just don't like him 'cause he isn't nice to you. If I'd been in an accident like him, I'd still be convalescing down at Hot Springs, or someplace like that. As far as I can tell, he doesn't feel the least bit sorry for himself, or want my sympathy at all. He sure didn't on the tennis court. All he says he's looking for is some way—any way—to get Kate off his back."

"You're so naive," said Malcolm, loftily. He gave a sort of chuckle. "Can't you see he's putting on an act? He thinks he's . . . what's-his-name? James Dean. *And* Axl Rose. The two of them rolled up in one. It's the old me-against-society thing. But all *he* ends up being is pathetic."

I hardly could believe how pompous Malcolm sounded, like a much, much older person—stuffy and above-it-all, and so contemptuous, to boot. Not just of David, but of his old friend Allie, too. Even though I still considered D to be a classically obnoxious boor, when I heard him being patronized that way, all my tendencies to hug the underdog came boiling to the surface. My having had a glimpse of David, naked in the moonlight, also didn't hurt his cause at all.

"You know," I said to Allie, pointedly ignoring Mal, "I've been thinking about the question that we talked about this morning. Why Kate invited us all here? I came up with an intriguing possibility. She's thinking of having David put away. So she wanted some impartial outside witnesses to see how weird he is."

Allie, I could see, took my suggestion seriously. Oh, she didn't look convinced or anything, but I could tell that she was thinking, and *considering*.

Malcolm, on the other hand, didn't think at all. Instead, he started running off his mouth, still in that uptown tone of voice of his.

"Good God," he started, and continued very much as if he was conversing with Him/Her, although he looked at Allison. "Will you listen to our friend Agatha Christie, Junior, here, making up another of her little stories." He moved his head and let his glance bounce off my shoulder. "Come off it, will you, Fleesh? That's just absurd. *You* know Kate—not well, but well enough. She's not that type of person. If you'd begin to pay attention to the simple, boring, everyday realities of life around here, you'd see that

David is a simple shithead, and Kate's just trying to make the best of him. And you'd quit this stupid overdramatizing you've been doing, and be—"

"What I'm *doing,*" I broke in to say, "is keeping what is called an 'open mind'—in case you've ever heard of one. And what I'm *not* doing is a lot of stupid stereotyping, and cramming everyone—including so-called friends of mine—into the little pigeonholes I've made for them." I was quite aware that I was sounding really pissed. That's what I *was*.

Malcolm looked, first, horrified, then chastened.

"Hey, easy does it," he began. You could see him switching gears. He even painted on a cozy little just-for-you type smile. "David isn't worth a squabble, honey. And you know that you *artistes*"—he gave it a French spin—"do tend to more or less imagine things sometimes." He reached out to give my foot a pat, the one that I had hanging off the bed. "That's why it's good for you to have a dull but basically well-meaning guy like me around—to keep things on a *reasonably* even keel." He'd made his voice particularly guy-like for that last part. *You* know, sounding like The Man in Charge.

A part of me still felt like kicking . . . oh, his patronizing, "friendly" hand, for openers, but I restrained myself. I wasn't ready yet (I didn't think) to end it all between us. After all, I'd tolerated Justin Sargent for a span of *months,* and he was much less fun to spend my time with, whether I was home or visiting, in a silly mood or serious, vertical or horizontal. And, for a rather shocking millisecond there, I had (which I had never felt before) a sense of power over an attractive boy. Could this be (I asked myself) a preview of a thing I long had hoped for—of how it feels (sometimes) to be a *woman*?

"Well," I said, perhaps a little haughtily, but angrily no more. I sat up straighter on the bed, but managed to look down at him while doing so, my lips a-flicker with a small suggestion of a smile.

"What *we've* decided," I went on, clearly meaning Allie and myself, "is that we're going to bring this up with Kate. Tonight, while she and Al are making dinner—it's homemade spaghetti sauce, oh, yum—providing David's not around, which he probably won't be. You"—I nodded down at Mal—"will certainly be welcome, if you want to come. *I* think it'd be good to have all three of us observing her. *And* hearing what she has to say." I put sweet reason in my voice. "You're right in thinking that the chances are his story is made up." I switched back to businesslike. "*But*—we think we ought to check it out. And so we're going to."

Malcolm nodded. Apparently, he'd climbed down off his high horse altogether; *that's the boy,* I thought.

"Okay," he said. "I understand. I've got to run up to my house a minute. That's if I can use your car, great benefactress." He aimed that at Al; she nodded. "But I ought to make it back for most of the"—he smiled—"investigation. I'm almost sure that Kate'll set your minds at rest. And I promise I won't say, 'I told you so.' "

"You'd *better* not," said Allie. She sounded slightly edgy still. "It isn't like we're saying we *believe* what David said, you know."

"I know," said Malcolm, smoothly, getting to his feet. "Oh, and by the way," he added, terribly offhandedly, "I stopped by the car center on the way back from school. I can get *my* car tomorrow—assuming I can get my dad to write a check today. So, I'm thinking that I'll move back home this weekend. . . ."

"Leaving Fleesh and me all by our *lonesomes*?" Allie said. You had to know her very well to know that underneath the whiny voice she'd used—put on—to say that line, she was really mad. *I* could see that in the way her foot twitched on the bed, and how she wrinkled up her nose, but I was pretty sure *he* couldn't read those signs.

"Well, we've got news for *you,* big boy," she then informed him. "We *already* decided *we* were leaving Friday afternoon. I'm staying at the Gordons for the weekend, and then Monday Thalia's coming back. I wouldn't think of leaving her up home alone."

What Allie'd said was partly true, at least. We *had* discussed our pulling out of Mycroft House—no matter how our talk with Kate turned out—but not without first finding out when *he* would like to leave. In *our* conversation, the three of us had still been musketeers. But now Allie was showing him that we could be as . . . *unilateral* (duolateral?) as anyone, I guess. I thoroughly approved. We both knew my mom was always glad to put up Allison. She'd even told her she could stay in Michael's precious room (you'd think it was a *shrine*), anytime she'd had an overdose of me.

"Good," said Mal, unfazed and oozing affability. "That's great. I'm sorry if I overreacted about David. I'm sure that his not liking me—just as you said—had lots to do with that. But, in spite of everything, I think we've had a ball here. I know *I* have. All thanks to you guys."

He smiled at both of us as he said that, but especially at me.

"And who's to say," he added, "that we won't soon have even a better one?"

Later on, I wondered how I looked right then. My sense of power had gone south, and I was feeling overmatched again. The woman I had briefly (maybe) been reverted to the girl too inexperienced to trust her feelings. Minutes before, Malcolm had acted like a highfalutin *rat*—until he'd met some real resistance and resentment. Then it seemed as if he'd backed right down and become increasingly agreeable, much like his "old self." But *then* he'd calmly sprung the news on us—on me—that he was leaving Mycroft House, and on a day he'd picked, to suit his selfish purposes—because his *car* was ready.

And finally, here he'd just apologized for everything (except his autocentric attitude), and then come on to me again, full blast, as if he just *assumed* that everything was great between us—and probably would get still better! As soon as he could get those condoms from the Beamer's glove compartment, maybe. (Or I could hurry up and make it to the drugstore.)

Luckily for me, he'd headed for the door. I looked at Allie; she looked back at me and made a face.

"Men," I said. But with a little (shameful) question in my voice.

"Malcolm," Allie said, emphatically.

Sixteen

Al and I were early getting downstairs to the kitchen, to begin the dinner prep. It wasn't that we couldn't *wait* to get our hands on big chef's knives, and vegetables that we'd chop up, sauté, and toss into the fresh tomato sauce we planned to make. Nor were we in a *tearing* rush to fry up little chunks of hot Italian sausage, or the pound of lean ground turkey Kate had said she'd gotten at the store. And although making up our minds about how much of which dried herbs we'd use would be enjoyable enough, *that* was (also) not the reason for our super-punctuality.

No, we left the second floor because we couldn't stand the waiting any longer. We wanted to get started on our questioning of Kate. We wanted it to be all over with. We wanted happy endings, or at least *an* ending of some sort, a resolution. We had to get this whole thing sorted out, and understood, and put behind us.

Coming down the stairs, we were as jumpy as a pair of feral cats; creaks that we'd ignored for days and days alarmed us. I'd taken a shower, and afterward smeared on the Speed Stick with a heavy hand—sort of how my dad does with his driveway sealer. But even then, I didn't feel secure and confident.

Kate wasn't in the kitchen yet, when we got down—no surprise to us, of course. So, Al and I just stood beside each other in that big room for a moment, looking all around and sort of reinforcing our decision; it *was* the perfect place for what we had in mind.

"If David gets the bright idea he wants to come and help," said Allison, "we'll see him coming down the hall, or hear him on the back porch, there."

"He isn't really interested in cooking," I opined. "He only *said* that, that one time."

"Let's go and see where Kate is," Allie said. So, off we wandered, through the dining room, into the living room and hall, and finally out onto the patio. There she was, in boots and dirty jeans, stretched out on a chaise, big glasses on her nose, a magazine in hand.

"Fleesh *insisted* she should help us with the sauce," said Allison. "She said her blood is three-eighths olive oil and garlic, on her mother's side."

"Is it that time already?" Kate looked at her watch. "Just about, I guess. But if we were gen-u-wine Italian chefs, we'd have started *yesterday,* I bet. Had the flavors marrying all night. *Ca-peetch,* Fuh-leetch-ee-a?"

"Rigatoni," I agreed, digging deep into my tiny store of real Italian words.

Kate nodded, sighed, and closed her magazine.

"I'll just wash up," she said, and stood. "And meet you in the kitchen. I was showing little brother how to make a fieldstone terrace, down beside that shack of his."

"Oh, yeah, I saw the stones laid out," I said, all innocence. "It looked like quite a job, to me. You think he'll get it done by dinnertime?" By then the three of us were in the center hall.

"Who knows?" Kate said. "It's hard to tell, with him. Sometimes he sticks with stuff right to the bitter end. Other times he says to hell with it and quits in half an hour. You never know, with him. I'm trying to sell him on the golden mean—a happy medium." She started up the stairs.

"Makes sense," I said. And, "See you in the kitchen, then."

Allison, for her part, said "Good *luck,*" but nowhere loud enough for Kate to hear her.

We'd arranged, beforehand, that Allie'd be the one who'd hit Kate with the story David told her. *I* said I'd throw in . . . remarks, supportive observations, underlinings. Just so she wouldn't feel that she was giving a soliloquy, or something. We didn't want to come across as prosecutors. We were more a pair of young Miss Marples, making certain . . . inquiries.

I don't know about Allie, but the reason *I* got out one of

the big knives right away, and started chopping celery and onions was that . . . well, I had the urge to practice chopping. It wasn't that I felt the need to *arm* myself, or anything. I wasn't *scared* of Kate or David. Not exactly, anyway.

Allie, probably, felt very much the same. Carrots and tomatoes were *her* raw material. The knives at Mycroft House were far superior to those we had at home: bigger, better balanced, and with a much, much keener edge. And they had no-slip grips, even in a sweaty hand.

"Hey—*I'm* impressed," said Kate, when she came in the kitchen. "You look like Culinary Institute instructors, doing that. So, what should *I* do? Fry a little sauce meat? Get those skillets smokin'?"

Allison and I agreed, shooting glances back and forth. Kate's cheerfulness was making this more difficult, I thought. But still, I jerked my head in her direction—she had her back turned, opening the fridge—while waggling my eyebrows. What I was telling Al, of course, was: Do it! Now! Begin!

"Uh—Kate. I had a talk with David yesterday," she started. "Actually, last night. Or, *actually*"—she gave a nervous little laugh—"*he* talked to *me*. I told Fleesh what he said, this afternoon, and she—well, both of us agreed we ought to talk to you about it."

Kate had straightened up and turned around by then. She had the thing of sausages in one hand, the ground turkey in the other; both were plastic-wrapped. The refrigerator door closed automatically, and almost silently, behind her.

"Oh?" she said. She looked from Al to me and back again. The chill was unmistakable. It was as if the air inside the refrigerator had escaped and spread throughout the room.

“Yup,” said Allie. Her eyes were on the stuff that she was chopping. She was being careful not to cut herself, I guess.

“*He* said,” she said, “that when he had that accident, he wasn’t by himself, that someone else was in the car, a girl. And that this girl was *killed,* and you helped him cover up her death. That *you* were the one who buried her, or something, so nobody would ever know what happened.”

I’d suspended operations as soon as Allison began to talk. I wanted to watch Kate, and see how she reacted. I didn’t put my knife down, though.

It seemed to me she looked more disappointed and annoyed than shocked, or . . . *guilty*. She gave the meat a toss onto the counter by the stove; she pursed her lips, then took a breath, and sighed. And shook her head. *Aha,* I thought; *denial*. And Allie hadn’t even gotten to the blackmail part.

“I suppose he told you that was how he cut his wrists,” she said, now sounding bitter and sarcastic, and (I hate to say it, but) *unfriendly*. “When he tried, unselfishly—hey, how about heroically?—to save her.”

Allie raised her head to look at me. It was a “How about it?” look, I thought, so I responded.

“He explained to Al he cut his wrists escaping from the car,” I said. “And he said he got the girl out, too. I don’t think he thought that made him any kind of hero, though.” Allie gave a little nod, when I said that.

“I suppose I shouldn’t be surprised,” said Kate, “but still I sort of am. I always try to tell myself he’s getting better. Not just on the surface, but deep down. What you heard from him, I’m sorry to say”—she looked at Allie—“was not only typical, but classical. It’s part of what’s so wrong with him, this adamant refusal to accept reality . . . and take responsibility. To tell it like it is, or was. In other words, to stop the fantasizing and the lying."

I didn't get what she was saying. What, exactly, was that meant to mean?

"You're saying that there wasn't any girl?" I said to her. "You're saying that he's lying?" Perry Mason had replaced Miss Marple.

"Oh, it's not exactly *lying,* in the regular sense of the word," Kate replied. "The story that he told you is a symptom. Possibly he thinks it's true, or did while he was telling it. He denies reality in lots of ways. It's easier—more comfortable—for him to hide behind the stories he makes up, or the different acts that he puts on. We all do pretty much what he does, I suppose, but on a smaller scale and usually for some specific purpose. But when *I* tell people a story—like the one I told you two and Malcolm, days ago—I know exactly what I'm doing, and I have a worthwhile end in mind. There's—as the saying goes—'a method to my madness.' " And she gave a little chuckle.

"The *story* you told us?" I said. "Which one was *that*?"

Now she looked discomforted. She stepped up closer to the counter and started picking at the wrapping on the pack of sausages.

"The one about the accident, of course." She sort of mumbled that. "That was a lie."

"Wait," said Allison. "You're saying that your version of the accident wasn't the truth? And you're also saying that David's isn't, either?"

"Or are you saying that there wasn't any accident at all?" said I.

"Not that kind of one," said Kate. She shook her head again, still looking at the meat in front of her. "Oh, God, I didn't want to tell you this, but now I guess I have to." She paused, as if to get her thoughts together. I started chopping up another onion; I was being cool.

"David has been sick a long, long time," she told us, speaking quietly and flatly. Out of the corner of my eye, I watched her head turn, looking first at Allie, then at me. "Since he was pretty young, I guess. Being so much older, I was away a lot—most of the time, when he was growing up—but I do remember hearing stuff about his temper, and the trouble he got in at school. And, even to me, he seemed pretty . . . *temperamental,* I guess you'd say. My parents tried to explain a lot of it away, saying he was hyperactive and a gifted child who just got bored a lot. And that they were probably too old to cope with him effectively. All of that might even have been true at first. But eventually, they had to face the fact that he had problems. They took him to a lot of different doctors, and they tried some special schools. Sometimes, I guess he seemed to have improved, but then he'd have a setback of some sort. *Physically,* he always thrived. There isn't a game or a sport he can't excel at, although he doesn't like to practice anything too long. But emotionally, he was all over the place. And when he reached the age of twelve, I think it was—the beginning of puberty, I guess—he started threatening to kill himself. Over a year ago—and no, it wasn't any accident—he slit his wrists. That's when he got those scars you've seen. It happened in my parents' house, and not in any car."

I don't mind admitting I was rocked when I heard that. Although I'd told myself—and later Allison—the exact same thing, I'd never actually *believed* it, do you know what I mean? It was just—as the saying goes—a *thought.* But, now . . . Here it was, a *fact,* from David's sister.

But then I had to catch myself. Kate, according to her own description of herself, "told stories." Had we just heard another one?

"My parents took it very hard, when he did that," she now was saying. "My mother had a nervous breakdown. So, at that point, I stepped in. My parents moved to Scottsdale, and I became his—David's—keeper, so to speak." She smiled a crooked smile.

"Well, I'd read—in *Time,* I think it was—about a brand-new kind of therapy," she said. "It was founded on the belief that a lot of so-called crazy, schizophrenic people—particularly kids—*aren't* crazy-schizophrenic. They have a choice; they don't *have to* act outrageously, the way they do. And that what they need, in addition to professional counseling and often some drugs, is to be around people who treat them 'normally'—as if they're in control, responsible, like all the rest of us. As if they're capable of choosing sanity, in other words. Well, I got in touch with a psychiatrist who believed in this method, and he agreed to work with David and with me. Me in the role of his main helper. I learned that I could say to him, 'Stop acting crazy,' and he would. Most of the time, at least. And it was this same doctor who thought that having other kids around him might turn out to be a big help, too. Not kids with problems, like the ones in special schools. Just *ordinary* kids, like you." She flashed that little smile again. "*You* know what I mean."

She started to unwrap the sausages, tearing off their plastic wrap.

I looked at Allie. I felt as if I needed to confer with her. Was she buying this new story? What should we do now? Should one of us bring up that we were leaving Mycroft House quite soon, all three of us?

Al looked back at me. But then her eyes moved, darted past my head. And, I swear, her skin lost what I'd call its ordinary healthy glow, and went all dull and flat, and even tightened up, across her cheekbones.

"Hi," she said, but not to me. I turned around. To David. He was standing in the pantry door. I assumed he'd been inside the pantry all this time. I hit my mental rewind button, trying to recall exactly what I'd said since we came in the kitchen. But it seemed the tape had been erased, somehow.

Seventeen

"Well, hi," he said. He seemed to be unfazed, extremely calm. He stuck both hands way deep inside the pockets of his pants and lounged against the pantry doorway. I released the breath that I discovered I'd been holding.

"I was back in there when you came in," he said. He tossed his head back toward the pantry. "Lookin' for some munchies. Workin' on that terrace, I got starved."

I took a peek at Kate while he was talking. She was holding the opened package of sausages, still, but she probably didn't know it. She was staring at her brother, *concentrating on him* is the way it seemed to me, the way she'd do if she was *willing* him to do or say something she had in mind.

He was looking everywhere but at his sister. His eyes went back and forth between my face and Allison's and, yes, the stove and the refrigerator, never settling on anything or anybody. I was reminded of the first time we met, and how he'd never looked at me for long, unless my back was turned. But his body language, now, insisted he was totally relaxed, at ease.

Because no one else was saying anything, I did.

"Kate said that you were doing that," I babbled. "Working on the terrace. I'll bet it's looking good, down there."

He smiled—or at least his mouth got wider, and he showed his even teeth.

"Oh, it *is,*" he said. "It absolutely *does.* You'll have to check it out. You and—no, forget it. But it's *really* atmospheric now."

I nodded stupidly, with matching grin in place.

"But, movin' on . . ." he said. Now his eyes were more on Allison than me. "I heard what you two said to sister Kate. And all that *she* said back. It was pretty interesting to me. I wasn't real surprised at all." He shifted his weight from one foot to the other, and leaned his head back, up against the door frame.

"Now it's my turn, though." He said that slowly, now looking intently at the upper corner of the pantry door. He paused, then turned his head to lock his eyes on Allie. I could see his hands turn into fists, inside his pockets.

"Now I've got to tell you *everything,*" he said. "I wasn't going to, ever, but I *got to,* now." He nodded slowly, four or five times, and when he stopped, he had his head bowed, looking at the ground with his eyes narrowed, the way a person does if he's trying to remember something.

"I have to clear my name," he said, and picked his head up, looking pleased.

(What was I thinking, listening to him? One main thing: Is he crazy; is he acting crazy *now*? Plus, I guess, the logical next question: Crazy or not, is he going to try to hurt someone?)

"The story I told *you,*" he said to Allison, "was *almost* the whole truth. I just left out some things—two itty-bitty little things. I had my reasons. People always have their reasons, don't they? *You* know Kate's." He shook his head and made a little laughing sound, as if he found that whole idea ridiculous—or maybe just too obvious for words.

"Yep," he said, and stared down at the floor again. "I had my reasons. For never telling anyone she wasn't dead—the girl I had with me that night. When I pulled her out, and got her to the shore, she wasn't dead at all. She was *hurt,* all right." He was speaking softly, and his head went forward, bearing down on "hurt." His eyes were seeing something far away from Mycroft House, I thought.

"She was hurt and she was *scared,*" he said, and made another head bob. "She said she couldn't move, except her hands and arms a little. I left her lyin' on the riverbank and told her I'd get help. Well, I got help for her, all right." He gave that little laugh of his again. "But not the kind she *thought* I'd get, I bet. She probably was real surprised she got the kind of help *I* sent her."

It was after he said that that he turned around and finally looked at Kate.

"You killed her, didn't you?" he said. His voice got very

soft and sounded strained. "You thought *I* thought that she was dead, so you just killed her. And me, I never questioned you. I never asked you what you did, down by the river. I had my reasons for that, too. I didn't want to know. It made me sick to think about it, even. It still does."

He shook his head, then cleared his throat and made that hawking sound that people make before they spit, and *spat,* right on the kitchen floor, just past the pantry door. I'd never seen a person do that—spit right on a *floor*—before. There was a shiny blob of it, right there on the linoleum.

"That's what I think of *you,*" he said to Kate, now sounding furious, and full of hate. He turned to Allison. "And you, too, Judasina." He sounded less convinced when he said that.

Then he looked at me and smiled that lunaticky smile of his again. "You," he said, "you don't even count. You're just in the crowd scene. You and that conceited creep you've taken such a shine to, that Paul *Simonize.*"

You won't believe what I did then, when I heard that. I giggled. It was mostly nervousness, of course. I never would have giggled if I hadn't been so nervous. Let's face it—what he said was not that funny.

But I guess, for me, the atmosphere was real close to unbearable. David had made an awful accusation; according to him, his sister wasn't only an extortioner, she also was a murderess. And he'd actually spat on the floor! I don't know if it was my mother's genes kicking in again, or what, but his doing something . . . well, as gross and off-the-wall as that, had made me more alarmed than anything.

And, in addition, there was still The Question: Who did I believe? Kate's David-as-a-suicidal-nut-case story had attracted me at first; it made me look so wonderfully *perceptive*. But I couldn't lose this thought: She'd lied to us before, for not that good a reason, so it could be she was lying now. And if she *had* done what he'd said she did . . .

On the basis of my contact with the two of them, Kate would be the one that I'd believe, no doubt about it—just like Malcolm said. But I had to factor in this thing that Allie'd had with David. Sure, she'd said that it was just a fling and purely physical, but still. Allison did *not*—would never—play around with crazy people. In my mind, that was just a *fact* about the girl. *Impetuous* she was, for sure. But foolhardy? Or self-deluding? *Never*.

So, there I was, standing in this kitchen, biting back on giggles and clutching this huge carving knife, and thinking that possibly I should be terrified of someone, but pretty much uncertain as to *who*.

"You know you don't believe a word of that," Kate was saying to her brother now. "You know that everything you've said is totally made up. And those are not your real opinions of the three of us at all." Amazingly, she spoke in what I'd have to call a cheerful tone of voice. Although she was flatly contradicting him, she wasn't sounding . . . confrontational at all. It could have been a comment on the weather she'd just made. While she spoke, she'd lined up all the sausages, side by side, in one big skillet.

"And as for spitting on the floor, come *on*. . . ." She shook her head.

"Don't start. . . ." he started, holding up a hand.

But she'd just paused to take a breath; she never really stopped.

"Here's what *really* happened," Kate went on. "You made up a story for a purpose. Maybe you'd been outside, somewhere, the day I told that fib of mine, out on the patio. And you overheard and thought: Hey, I can *use* that. You'd seen that Allison is very pretty, and you needed some way to . . . attract her interest, and her *sympathy,* perhaps. That's very understandable, and I don't blame you. That'd be a normal thing for any boy to want to do. I'm sure that Allison is always hearing *lines* from different boys. That's just the way it is, right, Allie?"

I looked at Al. By then, the giggle-urge had left me. She still seemed very pale; even her lips had lost their normal color. She was also still kind of staring at David, but as the question she'd been asked sank in, her head began to turn in Kate's direction. Her eyes looked very wide.

"No, you don't," said David to his sister, loudly. "That's—what you said—that's not the way it was at all. You think you're so damn smart; you don't know *anything.* I never had to try to hit on Allison. We got along together right away. It was just a fun deal, nothing serious. And none of you damn smarties knew about it, what the two of us were doin'. The truth is, she's been ballin' me for days and days and days—we had a *lot* of fun!" He laughed. I looked at Allison again. She now was staring at the floor, just looking miserable. "So, don't you start in tryin' to tell me what I think, or what I do, 'cause what you know adds up to zip-o, zero, nothin'!"

"Why don't you cut it out?" said Kate right back at him, still in a friendly tone of voice, but sounding firmer now. She reached out, as if to turn the gas on underneath the skillet, but then she seemed to change her mind; her hand dropped to her side again.

"We've heard enough," she said. "There's no point adding onto it. You know *I* know you're putting on an act. I *know* you, David. The longer you keep going with this, the more upset you're going to be—you know that, too. But you don't have to keep on going; it's all right. *Nobody* believes you, David. *Everybody* knows you know exactly what you're doing—that you're just *acting* crazy. So, for the last time: Cut it out."

While she said that, I just felt more confused than ever. I hadn't *liked* what David had just said, about himself and Allison, but I'd believed it. Hell, I *knew* that it was true. Now I watched him fighting for control. His eyes were dancing all around the room. He'd take a breath, and look as if he was about to speak, and then he'd stop and shake his head, and seem to think some more. And then inhale again—and start the process over.

When the words came out at last, they came in bursts—the way you hear that automatic-weapons fire does.

"All right. Just wait a minute, wait. I've got it. Hear me out. You tell her, Allie. How about that, huh? Go ahead. You tell her what the real exact facts are, concerning . . ."

But just as he was blurting all that out, who comes strolling down the hall but Malcolm.

"Tell who what?" he asked, as he came in the kitchen. His tone of voice was bland but cheerful; he was clearly in a jolly mood. I bet myself that his "old man" had laid a nice big check on him.

I don't think his question was responsible for what happened next, but within a few seconds everybody else (except for me) began to talk, all of them at different volumes.

Allie wasn't audible at all. Her head was shaking, and her lips were moving, but I couldn't hear a word that she was saying. Just going by the way her head was turned, I'd say the person she was talking to was Kate.

I *did* hear part of what Kate said, to David, not to Allie. Her first few words were, "What I'm going to do is get your pills. . . ." But David, also hearing them, I guess, went totally bananas.

Of course, that's not a psychiatric diagnosis. All I mean is he got even more emotional and incoherent. He began to point at Kate, emphasizing different thoughts (none of which I fully understood) with rapid, jabbing gestures. What made him really difficult to understand was he was crying—*sobbing,* actually—perhaps hysterically, although I'm hardly competent to say.

Yet, through it all, I kind of got the message he was sending. It was pretty simple, actually. He hated her. He thought that she was evil. He called her all the awful words he knew; he didn't seem to care if they were relevant or not, or if he'd said them once already. He *did* look crazy then, with little shiny flecks of spittle shooting from his mouth, and his long hair, which had got undone, flying all around his head.

I'd never seen a boy come close to being that upset before, except perhaps one time before a fight began, right in the first-floor hall at school. Like then, I felt afraid. But not of him—of what was maybe going to happen.

Malcolm's contribution to this scene was to attempt to change it. Or, failing that, to understand it. He was yelling, "Hey, hold on! What's going on? Will someone tell me what the hell is happening?" I think he aimed that last at me.

Well, he could darn well *see* what happened next; I didn't have to tell him. David, with a final, tearful roar and gesture of disgust to all of us, ran across the kitchen to the back porch door, which he yanked open and went through, and then slammed emphatically behind him.

His going silenced everybody, briefly. Everybody clearly heard the car start up.

That activated us, of course. Out we all went, after him, muttering our questions, or our anger and concern. It wasn't that we thought we'd catch him; we just followed, doing *something*. We stopped together when we reached the front of Mycroft House, and saw that Allie's Mustang wasn't in the place where she and Malcolm always parked it.

Mal had left the keys in it, of course, as usual. He hadn't had a reason not to. But still, he started to apologize for doing so.

Allison began to wander down the driveway, in the direction that the car had gone, but when she'd taken twenty steps or so, she stopped. Then slowly started back, and stopped again. I went to stand beside her, and I'd just reached out to put my arm around her when we heard a siren in the distance.

Allie closed her eyes and just said, "Oh, my God," before she put her head down on my shoulder. Much, much later on, she swore to me she knew right then that he was dead.

Eighteen

He'd run the car into a big old maple tree, less than half a mile away. When he'd left the driveway, he'd turned right on Sycamore. When it dead-ended there at County Highway 49, the Richmond Pike, he'd made another right. The Pike curves left about a quarter of a mile beyond that point, but David kept on going straight. State Police investigators later said there weren't any skid marks on the road, and that the car had been traveling "well in excess of the posted speed limit," which at that point on the road was fifty.

Kate had gone inside the house, about the time we heard the sirens, saying she was going to call the town police. The three of us stayed out there on the driveway.

"What happened?" Malcolm asked again, coming up to us. "What was going on in there? Was it what you said to Kate that made him blow like that?"

I gave him a quick rundown, leaving out the David-Allie romance (if you want to call it that). Malcolm nodded sagely. It was pretty dark out there, and of course we hadn't yet been told what happened. In fairness to him, I ought to say I'm sure he thought that Allie was just feeling bad because her car'd been stolen.

"Well, remember I said I'd asked my dad to check out David's story? What he found out was that our boy was far from being Mr. Popularity—or even Mr. Normal High School Joe—in Marshville, Indiana," he began. "In fact, he always went away to school, so no one knew him all that well. But there *were* a lot of stories, none of which Dad's sources could confirm. Apparently, his family could hush up things they didn't want becoming public knowledge." And at that point, I think he actually smiled.

"Much as I hate to say this, knowing how it's liable to pump up Fleesh's ego, there *was* a real strong rumor that he'd tried to kill himself one time." I saw him shake his head. "Just as you said."

We heard the front door close and turned to see Kate coming toward us. I remember thinking she looked cold; then we saw that she was crying.

"There was an accident," she told us, speaking haltingly, her hands clasped together near her chest. "Out on the Pike. A red Mustang . . . hit a tree, head on. They wouldn't tell me, but they're coming over. I'm sure he must be dead. My poor, poor David's dead."

I really felt my knee joints get all watery, the way you read about. But then I realized I was holding on to Al; my focus shifted, off of me and onto her and Kate.

Mal went to Kate at once, and he was perfect. He seemed to somehow *know* just what to say and do. Allison and I were crying, too. The four of us went back inside together. Malcolm put us in the sitting room and made us all sit down. He found a box of Kleenex somewhere. He even went and got some brandy and four little glasses, though nobody wanted any.

"The police will be here any minute," Kate said then. Her eyes were red and swollen and still full of tears. She blew her nose. "Could we *not* go into all that . . . *stuff* with them? Could we just say he *borrowed* Allie's car—to go and get some ice cream?"

"I don't care. That's fine. Say anything," said Al. She was beside me on the sofa, leaning forward, with her face still partly in her hands.

I tried to think—imagine—what my mother'd say if she were there, in my place. *Don't make unnecessary waves* was one good possibility. "Sure," I said. "It doesn't matter."

"I felt so sorry for the guy," said Mal the hypocrite. "May he rest in peace, is what *I* say."

The town police did not stay long. They were regretful, and considerate of all of us. They were sure he'd died on impact. I got the feeling that they hadn't been inside "the Grunfeld House" before, the way they looked around.

It was an awful evening, just as you'd expect. Kate had a lot of calls she had to make, and said there wasn't anything that we could do for her, but that she was thankful we were there. When it was just the three of us, alone, Malcolm started sending up these verbal trial balloons, trying to ascertain how Al and I would feel if he pulled out and headed home the next day. He said his parents sort of had

been "counting on" his getting back.

Allie was real quiet. When she spoke, it usually was just to say—repeat—how "unbelievable" this was, how she could simply not believe that he was dead. I shared that feeling with her, though in a different way, I'm sure. My focus was on Allison. I wanted just to hold her, tell her everything would be all right. I got her to the kitchen, where I made some sandwiches for everyone, and put away the stuff that we'd been getting ready for our sauce. The sausages I sniffed at, and then threw away. Malcolm said the sandwiches were "fabulous"; he wolfed down two. Allie ate a half of one, probably not even knowing she was doing that. A little later on, I went upstairs with her. Mal said he'd look for Kate and maybe take some food to her.

When we got to Allie's room, she asked me to come in. I said of course; I wanted to.

"This is so weird," she said, when we had settled on the bed. "You know I didn't think of him as, like, my *boyfriend*. Not at any time. I *told* you; it was just a fling. But now—it's crazy—it's as if he was, had been. You know? D'you suppose I really loved him, Fleesh?" Her eyes were full of tears again.

"I don't know," I said. I was confused. In most of my encounters with him, he had been . . . *obnoxious* (you could say—*I* always did). But yet, somehow, that hadn't made me hate him. In fact, and now in retrospect, it seemed I'd sort of *liked* him. He'd been different, and he *was* attractive, physically. And he *had* told Kate he liked me, that one time. If *I* had slept with him (I thought), I bet *I* would have loved him.

"You could have, easily," I said to Al. "I always felt that he was really . . . *sweet* inside." And then I said one of those things that people always say about a person that they're feeling dual about. "I think that, basically, he lacked self-confidence, is all."

Allie nodded. "Oh, I *know* that's right," she said. And I could see her eyes go far away and back in time, as she remembered something.

"His story of the accident, and all," she said, a moment later, "that must have been a total fantasy. He lived in two completely different worlds, I guess, and one of them was all made up. Kate was telling us the truth. He'd tried to kill himself before, and this time he succeeded. He really had no confidence at all."

She stated all of that as fact. This was Allie saying he was crazy, had been all along, as if she'd known it all along. But still, I had the feeling she was asking me a question, or *some* questions that came down to one: Who'd been telling us the truth?

The answer in my heart was: I don't know.

But what I said was, "Yes, that's right," with as much certainty as I could muster. That was the best way for it to be. The other way was just too horrible to contemplate—or *deal with:* that *he* had told the basic truth, and that his sister, Kate, was *twice* a murderess. Of a girl, directly, and, in a sense, of him.

Either way, of course, one thing was indisputable: David Mycroft now was dead, and *nothing* that we thought, opined, or even proved would ever bring him back again.

Mal did move out, next day, telling Kate his mother needed him at home to serve as chauffeur for his little sister,

Sally; some surgery his mom was having on her foot was making it impossible for her to drive, and his dad had just left town on business. For all I knew, that could have been the truth—*all* that. He said he would "look in on us" from time to time.

Al and I stayed on until the weekend, when we moved to my house; my parents had agreed that staying until then would be the "thoughtful thing to do," when I called up to let them know about the "accident." Malcolm did come by the first three nights he was back home, but I think he felt a little . . . *I* don't know, either guilty or at least out of the flow. David was cremated on the second afternoon; we went with Kate to a little service beforehand; Mal didn't know about it. And Kate and Allie and I were having other conversations that he wasn't in on; we were being David-centered, still, while he was picking up the threads of ordinary life. I guess I wasn't too responsive to his invitations to "run out and get a cone," or "take a little stroll." At school, he asked if anything was "wrong." I think I said, "*Aside* from David getting killed?", which made him get all huffy. Kate took David's ashes back to Indiana, on the day we left the house.

Of course, when I was by myself, at night, all sorts of things went through my mind—scenarios and plot lines, possibilities galore. But I never brought them up with Allie, nor did I follow up in any way, alone. I decided that I'd just *assume* that Kate and David's parents were alive, and living out in Scottsdale, Arizona, and that David hadn't tried to kill himself by driving off a bridge back home.

Naturally, I also thought about myself a lot. (I hope that "naturally" is right, and that I wasn't being grossly egocentric.) It seemed incredible that just a few short weeks before I'd absolutely *hungered* for experience. I suppose I'd thought—except I didn't really *think* at all—that all "experience" was vaguely (or entirely) glamorous, like going on a trip abroad and hiking in the Scottish highlands, or living in a Cretan village for a while, or making steamy love with a Parisian sculptor in his huge, high-ceilinged atelier, which smelled of spilled red wine and cabbage soup. Could I have been that stupid?

The facts, of course, are otherwise. Experience is also disillusionment—take, for instance, the roller-coaster ride I'd had with Malcolm Warren. Experience is when you see that *life,* unlike a story, can't be plotted, rearranged, revised to suit one's fancy. Experience is finding out that every question doesn't have an answer. Experience is learning that the best intentions aren't guarantors of good results.

I'd never known a person my own age to die, before. Although I'd known that this could happen, I guess I never thought it *would*. And, *especially,* I'd never thought a person my own age would die, and I would be responsible—*somewhat* responsible, *a little bit* responsible. Or, put it this way: that if I hadn't *existed,* it was possible that the person might be still alive.

The thing is that I *did* insist to Allie that we had to talk to Kate. And I *did,* as I recall, propose that we should do that talking in the kitchen. And it's certainly true that if we hadn't talked to Kate, and in the kitchen, David would probably be still alive, today.

But what I *also* realized, thank God (we talked this out together, Al and I), was that were I to *blame* myself, on grounds like that, I would also have to blame Kate's parents, Kate, David himself, Al and Mal, several psychiatrists, and even Ms. Kevorkian. All of us, in one way or another, helped to set this tragedy in motion. Yet none of us—or even all of us together—could properly be *blamed* for it. There wasn't any blaming to be done.

Experience is finding out that sometimes bad things happen, and all that we can do is cry and slowly make our peace with them.

I'm sure that Allison and I were changed by having spent that time at Mycroft House. I think we're less impulsive now, and less judgmental. More thankful for a lot of things, such as our health, and (even with their flaws) our families, and having friends like each other.

My writing? Well, I'm still into it, as much as or more than ever. And though my work is still imaginative, for sure, I try to keep imagination where it belongs—that is to say, in writing. I finished *Sanctuary*. I'm ashamed to say I didn't do a lot more work on it, but at least I brought it to an end. I wasn't "blocked"—nothing that dramatic, or pathetic. I simply lost my . . . I don't know, *commitment* to the story. But when I saw our due date fast approaching, I got my act together long enough to write a final chapter. It was pretty weak, albeit slightly satisfying—and most of all, abrupt.

In it, Annabel and Fee sat down and told each other everything that had been going on, in one room or another in that castle. This both amazed them and amused them greatly. At the end, they laughed and came to an agreement, thus:

"You know what *I* think?" said Fiona, lolling on the end of A.D. Day's magnificently unmade bed.

"Possibly. Perhaps. I'm not quite certain. *Say,*"

her friend replied. *She* was propped against the headboard of said bed.

"I think that other than . . . well, thee and me, Costner's Castle's guests are knaves and varlets," said Fiona, and she nodded once, for emphasis.

Annabel D. Day considered that, then smiled.

"Martin Silverado is a *definite* kuh-nave," she said. "And always has been, I suppose."

"If he had the chance, he'd do it *in* a nave, like of a church, and with a serving wench," Fee added. "And so might Dermott, I imagine."

"Yes," her friend agreed. "But Dermott's slightly different, more the varlet type. Amiable perhaps, but in a freeloading, seafaring, pathological liar kind of way."

"Whereas the Lady Marge . . ." said Fee.

"Is merely fruitcake batter-matter—nutty . . ."

". . . Cashew City."

"A bit too much to swallow, I should say."

"It sounds to me," said Fee, "as if you might be thinking the same as me."

"That it be time to hit the bricks?" said Annabel D. Day. "To head for our respective hearths and homes?"

"Precisely that," said Fee. "Except . . ."

"Except for what?" said Annabel.

"Well," Fiona said, "there *is* another being in the castle who is sane and sweet—like us—and who might absolutely *love* the thought of . . . sanctuary."

Annabel D. Day was not the type you had to draw a picture for.

"So, let's just ask her." And she gave the center of the bed a whack.

"Here, Grace," she said. "Come up and answer us a question."

The big brown dog hopped right up on the bed and looked at both her newfound friends in turn.

"Grace," Fiona Garland said, "I'm sure you heard what we've been saying. We've decided we have had enough of Costner's Castle, and we're going home. But we would love to have you join us, come and stay with both of us—*forever,* if you like. We'll be leaving any minute now, so if you *are* a bit bummed out, and possibly would enjoy a change . . . What say you?"

Grace's big brown head was up, her ears as well. She *looked* extremely interested. But to the girls' regret, she leaped right off the bed and ran directly out the door.

"Well, that's a sad surprise," said Annabel. "I really thought she would've—Oh, my gosh!"

For there was Grace again, now standing in the doorway, looking in at them and wagging her big tail. She'd gone and got, and now had in her mouth, her nice red nylon leash.

"I guess we're looking at a 'yes,' " said Fee, delightedly. And in the time it takes to cram a lot of stuff into two suitcases, the three of them were outside on the street, prancing off toward (as it happened) just the loveliest of sunsets.

Because she was, herself, a writer, Ms. Kevorkian could really understand how David's death had shocked me and disturbed me—knocked me for a loop, to tell the truth. I suspect that was the reason she forgave me such a rush job of an ending, and gave the rest of my brief manuscript a lot of raves, in class. "High outrageousness," she called it once.

Justin wanted very much to get his hands on it, of course; that was him, all over. What people "got," himself especially, was always on his mind. But I'm sure that you'll believe me when I say: I never let him touch, or even *see,* my lovely *A*.